CALLEVA ATREBATUM ⬚ AD 79 ⬚

NORTH GATE

EARTH RAMPARTS

AMPITHEATRE

ATREBATAN COMPOUND

CLAY PITS
TILEMAKER'S YARD

TILEMAKER

MOSAIC MAKER

WEST GATE

BASILICA

FORUM

EAST GATE

PROPOSED NEW ROAD

SACRED GROVE

PROPOSED NEW EAST GATE

BATHS

TEMPLE

TEMPLE

FORUM STREET

EARTH RAMPARTS

N
W E
S

PORT WAY TO OLD SARUM
(SORVIODUNUM ROAD)

SOUTH GATE

Chapter 1

Topher felt angry as he stood outside the terraced house in Lynton Road. A squall of cold air shook the FOR SALE sign. It was early September, but the sycamore trees were losing their yellow leaves. It's not fair, he thought. I've only just got used to thinking of this house as home. He and his dad had lived in Cambridge for less than a year. They'd lived in London before that. Then he and his dad – and Ka of course – had moved in with Molly. Now they were on the move again, worse luck, going south this time.

Molly was Topher's stepmother now, Ka his very special cat. She was waiting for him, thank goodness. He could see her inside looking out of the window, watching the leaves fall from the trees. No – he couldn't help smiling – she was watching him. Her mouth opened in a soundless *Miaow*. Open the door, Topher. Come inside. That's what she was saying. He took the key from his pocket, and let himself into the hall. First she rubbed against his legs in welcome. Then she leaped up the stairs to gaze at him adoringly. The railings framed her beautiful face. What a face! What a cat! Her honey-coloured fur was flecked with black and white. Her eyes changed with the changing light. Now her shiny black pupils were rimmed with amber. On her forehead the key-like ankh – the Egyptian sign of life – was shiny black too.

He stroked her throat and felt her purrs.
Tophe ... rrr! Don't wo ... rry.

'At least I've got you, Ka.'

As long as you don't go away, he thought but didn't say. He didn't want to put ideas in her head. She did go away sometimes, further than most people would believe or imagine. She was a time-travelling cat who had travelled to Ancient Egypt once – and so had he! He dumped his coat and bag on the floor, but didn't pick up the post. Molly would nag, but he didn't care. Most of the letters would be from estate agents anyway. Molly had changed lately in several ways. She'd had a good effect on his dad at first and used to be really kind and helpful. Now the two of them were impossible. All they thought of was keeping the house tidy, in case people came to see round it. And it was worse when strangers did come round. It was as if aliens had landed. Ka didn't like it either. When they arrived she shot upstairs. When they peered into Topher's bedroom she glared down at them from the top of the wardrobe – and looked as if she'd like to drop missiles on their heads.

Molly and his dad didn't care about his feelings at all. *Topher ... rrr. Be fai ... rrr.* Ka purred round his feet now and seemed to speak. Sometimes she did speak. That was another amazing thing about her. But she was being an ordinary cat now. As a shaft of sunlight filtered through from the kitchen, she gave a loud *Miaow*! Then her pupils narrowed and round amber eyes blazed at him, before she headed for the kitchen. He laughed at her tail held so proudly – like an exclamation mark! Her neat bum was the full stop beneath!

In the kitchen Buggins, Molly's cat, was fast asleep

on a pile of newspapers by the boiler. He was so fat he couldn't leap onto the boiler as Ka did.

'Hi, Buggins.'

The old tabby opened one eye, but didn't stir himself till Topher had filled both dishes. Then both cats ate side by side. Buggins didn't seem to have a strong territorial instinct or maybe he was too fat to do anything about it if he did. He'd accepted Ka's arrival without demur and now he hardly noticed the invading house-viewers.

At about six o'clock Chris Hope and Molly came in, Molly first, shaking rain off her long black hair. His dad was seconds later, his bald head wet and shiny. He was quite a bit older than Molly.

'Hello, Topher.'

'Hello, son.' Chris Hope took off his glasses to dry them.

'What weather!' said Molly.

They spoke cheerfully enough to Topher, but there was a strained atmosphere between them. It was worrying. Only a short time ago they'd been celebrating because they'd both got new jobs down south. Molly was a scientist doing research into cancer. His dad was a computer programmer. They'd been luvvy-duvvy when they were first married. Now it was as if there were taut wires between them. Was it his fault, for not being pleased about the move?

Over supper he said, 'I suppose I'll get used to it, the move I mean. Where did you say we were going?' He hadn't shown any interest before, but Molly hadn't nagged and she'd brought home pizza for supper. Pizza was his favourite. She knew that. 'And you did warn me, in a way,' he went on. 'You said we'd move to a bigger house when we sold the London one.'

Molly gave him a grateful smile, but she hardly ate any pizza and she was drinking water. But Molly usually loved food, and his dad usually opened red wine when they had pizza. What was wrong? His helpful remarks hadn't exactly cheered them up. But they did exchange one of those – shall we tell him? – looks. So he waited a bit, but neither of them said anything else, so he went upstairs to do his homework.

Ka didn't come up till later, till he was in bed in fact, finding it hard to get to sleep. She sprang onto his bed and rubbed her cheeks against his.

'Go away, cheesy breath!' She loved cheese and must have been eating left-over pizza. Fortunately she knew he didn't really want her to go away. After a bit, she burrowed under the bedclothes and settled against his stomach, purring.

Don't wo...rry.

Don't wo...rry.

He fell asleep quite soon after that, but in the morning he started worrying again. He heard Molly being sick in the bathroom.

As soon as he got home from school he rang Ellie. Ellie had been his best friend in London. He hadn't yet made another friend as good as her. He told her about Molly being sick and all the other things – and she laughed.

'Thicko! Isn't it obvious?'

'No.' He didn't like being called thicko even by Ellie, especially by Ellie in fact.

'She's pregnant, Topher!'

'Having a baby?'

'That's what pregnant means.'

He ignored her sarcasm. It was such a relief. He'd thought Molly was ill – and that she might die like his mum, who had died in an aeroplane crash. He'd only just got over that – to the extent that you ever get over something like that.

'Topher! Are you still there?'

'Yes.'

Ellie was reassuring. 'It'll be okay. Babies are okay. Noisy and smelly but okay. And Molly will be more normal in a few weeks.'

'In a few weeks!'

'Yes, Topher. Pregnancy is nine months from start to finish. The feeling sick stage usually lasts about two.'

She was very knowledgeable.

When Molly did tell Topher – about two weeks later – he told her that he'd guessed. She said she'd wanted to be sure before she told him. The two of them were having supper together. His dad was away.

'Touch wood – it will be a very understanding baby,' she said. 'This wasn't planned I'm afraid. I'm not sure I'll be any good with babies. I was quite happy with my ready-made family,' she added giving Topher a smile, but she still didn't look really happy. Touch wood. Not planned. Molly had changed. She'd be talking about horoscopes next.

*

Next day, a Saturday, she drove them both to Chichester which was nearly on the south coast – to meet his dad and start house-hunting. They arrived at lunchtime and ate in an Italian restaurant. Molly's appetite had returned – that was one good thing and they all ate big dishes of pasta. For pudding Topher had tiramisu, a chocolatey sort of trifle. Afterwards, while driving round to get the feel of the area, Topher picked up that Chichester was an important yachting centre – another good thing! He'd recently taken up sailing and turned out to be quite good at it. It was something he'd wanted to do ever since he'd met Sir Francis Drake on his last time-travelling expedition. With luck – and some cash from his dad – he'd be able to carry on with it.

They looked at several houses with FOR SALE signs outside them, from the outside. There were two very modern ones near the hexagon-shaped Festival theatre, a couple of Victorian ones and one Georgian. His dad went on a bit about the different kinds of architecture. He said Chichester had been important since Roman times – the main roads still followed the Roman plan in fact – and there was a Roman palace nearby. Topher asked if they were anywhere near Silchester, which he knew was down south somewhere. He'd read about a Roman tile with a cat's pawprint in it, which had been found there. There was a photo of it in one of his books and he'd always wanted to see it. His dad said they weren't very near Silchester, and ought to concentrate on house-hunting. But on the way home next day, Molly made a detour. It was to reward him for being Super

Child she said. While his dad drove straight back to Cambridge in his car, she drove to Reading. And there it was in Reading Museum, on display with other Roman stuff from Silchester – a reddish-brown tile with the pawprint in it! He could have put his fingers where the cat had put her paw – if the tile hadn't been covered with glass. *Her* paw! Why did he think that? Was this the pawprint of the first cat in Britain? The Romans had brought cats to Britain, most experts thought. Was this the paw of the great great great great grandmother of all British cats? Whose cat was she, and what had happened that day, when she pressed her paw into the wet clay?

As he stood wondering, Molly called him over to look at a bronze eagle, which was quite interesting. It was *the* symbol of Roman power, she said. It had been part of a statue that stood in the Forum of Calleva Atrebatum. In fact the Emperor had held it in his hand. Calleva was the Roman name for Silchester which was about twelve miles from Reading. The Atrebates were the tribe that the Romans had conquered, if conquered was the right word. Like most southern tribes, quite a lot of the Atrebates welcomed the Romans. They hadn't resisted them anyway. They'd taken the Buggins approach and settled for a quiet life!

When Molly apologised because they couldn't stop long, Topher said he was ready to go. The pawprint had made him worry about Ka. She was the sort of cat who disappeared for days on end sometimes and sometimes went too far. Sometimes she stayed away too long and got into terrible danger. Suddenly he wanted to feel her paws on his knee. He wanted to finger her fur and hear her purrs. As Molly drove home through the rain-filled darkness – windscreen wipers swishing away – he thought about his cat and hoped she would be waiting for him.

Chapter 2

It was still raining when they got home at just after 8 o'clock. As he walked up the front path, slippery now with fallen leaves, Topher wondered where Ka would be. A street lamp cast a yellow glow over the path making the puddles look like gold, but he didn't expect to see her sitting on the doorstep admiring the view. Ka didn't like wet weather. He was worried when his dad opened the door and said he hadn't seen her, though he'd been home for two hours. Quickly Topher checked all the rooms downstairs, then dashed upstairs to see if she was in his bedroom. When she wasn't there, he looked on his bedside table for the carving, that his mum had given him before she died. He didn't want to find it though.

The carving was a little cat statue made of sardonyx, a honey-gold stone flecked with black and white – Ka's colours. In fact the statue was Ka's double, a perfect replica which came to life sometimes! But only he knew that. Even Ellie hadn't understood when he tried to explain it once. She thought he was joking. So he searched for the carving anxiously, *not* wanting to find it, because if he did, he'd know that she was time-travelling. The carving was there only when Ka was in another time. It was as if she left a photo behind her, a three-dimensional photo, to remind him what she looked like. As if he could forget! When she was away he thought about her all the time, worried about her. People in the past often treated cats with terrible cruelty, even the Egyptians who worshipped them.

The carving wasn't on the table beside his bed, nor in the cupboard beneath it. Gently he shook his red bean-bag onto the grey carpet, because he'd found it there once, hidden in the folds. Then he looked behind the books on the bookshelf because Ellie had found it there once. She'd told him off for not looking after such a beautiful object. And as he searched, tidying up as he went along, his hopes rose – of not finding it – because if the carving wasn't in his room, then Ka was probably in the neighbourhood somewhere, wandering like an ordinary cat. It didn't take long to search his small room thoroughly, and after about ten minutes he went downstairs to the kitchen where his dad was making toasted sandwiches for supper. Through a doorway he could see Molly sitting by the gas-fire with her feet on a stool.

'No sign of Ka, Topher?' she called out.

Buggins was sitting in the chair opposite her.

'No.'

'Go and see if Mrs McCarthy has seen her – or ring.'

Topher had already thought of that. Mrs McCarthy was their next-door neighbour, who had been feeding the cats for them while they were away. When he rang, she said she'd last seen Ka a couple of hours earlier in the back garden. So he went outside first to the back then out the front – calling her name and banging her dish. But she still didn't appear. More worried now, he went inside again. She hadn't come back by the time he went to bed, and he found it hard to get to sleep. He always found sleeping difficult when Ka wasn't there. Hoping she'd come into his room later on, he read for a while and had another look at the Silchester pawprint in his *Encyclopaedia of the Cat*. It was a black and white photo but he could see it now in pinky red terracotta. There was quite a lot about the Romans in the encyclopaedia. It said that a Roman poet called Martial was the first person to call a cat *catta*. The more usual word was *feles* or *felis*. The Romans loved cats, and even named towns after them. Kattewyk in Holland, was first called Cat Vicense by the Romans. Cat Vicense means cat neighbourhood. Wherever the Roman army went, they took cats with them – to guard their corn supplies from rats and mice and bring them luck. The superstitious Romans probably brought cats from Egypt to Europe and might even have worshipped them like the Egyptians did. They definitely thought cats had healing powers. Oh no! 'Yuk! That's disgusting!' He didn't realise he'd spoken aloud till Molly put her head round the door and said, 'What's disgusting?'

He read out, '*Pliny, historian of the Roman Empire, considered cats' faeces to be medically effective. Mixed with mustard the dung was said to cure ulcers of the head. To draw out thorns, it was mixed to a thick paste with a little wine.*'

'You won't be wanting this one back then?'

She stepped into the room and there was Ka with her feet in the air. Molly was carrying her like a baby!

11

Ka stayed around, thank goodness. Life was unsettling enough without her going walkabout. He never knew when he'd find strangers peering into his room, saying what they'd do to it if it were theirs. So far they'd only looked at the house. No one had said they wanted to buy it, but it was only a matter of time before someone swept his things aside and installed their own. Molly and his dad were away quite a bit too – separately. They went to look at new houses or discuss their new jobs. At school it was hard to concentrate when people were planning things you wouldn't be there for. Once again he felt as if he didn't belong. The one quite good friend he'd made, Simon, seemed less friendly when he learned that Topher was moving.

One night in November his dad said, 'Well, Topher, we've found a nice house in a village outside Chichester, and a very good new school. See what you think.'

He handed Topher a brochure for a boys only private school called Noviomagus. Noviomagus was the Roman name for Chichester, Topher recalled, and the school seemed archaic. The boys wore blue and gold uniforms and went to school on Saturdays! He didn't fancy it at all – and said so. Last time at least he'd helped choose the school he went to.

'And that wasn't a great success, was it?' his dad said. 'You got in with the wrong set and academic progress was nil. This school is within walking distance of our new house, and the classes are small. It will be good for you.'

They set off the following Friday, to view house and school on the Saturday. Topher felt that it didn't matter what he thought. As they drove into the village on Saturday morning he caught a glimpse of the school entrance with boys streaming through it. Some of them were on bikes. Most were dropped off from cars. A board said

NOVIOMAGUS TRUST SCHOOL.
Founded 1894
Headmaster. Dr E. Warman MA, PhD

Red brick turrets were visible above the trees but there wasn't much else to see. Trees also surrounded Fletcher House, which was at the bottom of a long gravelled drive. Some climbing plant covered the brick walls. Double-fronted and detached with leaded windows, it was in a cul-de-sac called Fletcher's Close where there were about five other houses. His father parked the car in front of a stone porch with pillars on either side. The door looked as if it should have been in a castle. When they stepped across the entrance hall their feet sounded like an invading army's. There was a musty smell but only because the house was empty according to his dad – to whom the emptiness was a great attraction. It meant they could move in quite soon. Topher had four bedrooms to choose from. He chose the biggest, even though it had babyish paper on the walls. His dad said they'd get the decorators in straightaway. The room was at the back of the house overlooking the large garden where there was a swing hanging from a tree. A younger child must have lived here before.

Fortunately it was afternoon when they drove up to Noviomagus School, which had obviously been built by someone with delusions of grandeur. It was a red brick Victorian building with turrets and pinnacles, an imitation castle. Two stone lions flanked the flight of steps leading to the entrance. Topher was glad that the boys had gone home. At least he wouldn't be gawped at as he walked round the classrooms. The headmaster appeared in the doorway as soon as they parked the car. He looked like a Roman elder, Topher thought, as he looked down on them. His short hair was combed forward in the Roman style, his nose was hooked and his black gown was a bit like a toga. As soon as the introductions were over – there was a lot of Dr This and Dr That – he waved his arm and said, 'Let's begin the grand tour. Follow me!' Then, black gown billowing, he entered the octagonal entrance hall and led the way up a wide staircase. Topher, trogging behind, thought the classrooms on the first floor were dull and old fashioned. They had high windows, dusty blackboards and old desks in straight lines. It wasn't till they went outside to a newer building that he saw anything modern. But the language laboratories and the science block had all the latest equipment. As they drove back to the hotel his dad went on about them.

From then on things moved at a dizzying pace. Moving day was fixed for the first of December. For days previously the house was full of strangers doing the packing. Topher said he'd pack his own, but his dad said his new firm was paying all the removal expenses and the experts would do a better job. They would pack things carefully, he said, label them and put them in the right rooms when they got to the new house.

Ka hated the strangers. She spent a lot of time outside, sitting in the poplar tree at the bottom of the garden, even though the weather had turned wintry. One Friday she wasn't there – in house or garden – when Topher came home from school. She didn't come in that night and he found the statue in the cupboard beside his bed. She stayed away the whole of the weekend, worrying him a lot, but she was on his bed when he came home from school on the Monday and the statue had gone again.

'Where have you been, Ka?'

She was sniffing the packing cases, which housed most of his possessions now.

He picked her up and looked into her eyes.

'Tell me – where have you been?'

She struggled to get down, so he let her – and she went back to the cases. Only when she'd rubbed her cheeks against all of them did she settle beside him on the bed. Strangely, she wasn't as hungry as she usually was when she'd been away. She purred loudly and seemed contented.

'Where did you go?' He tried again. She didn't reply, except for loud purrs, and he wished he could get to his computer. She sometimes answered by writing on his computer, but it was in one of the cases. 'You don't have to go, escape to another time I mean. I'll look after you in the new place. It's got a big garden. You might even like it.'

Buggins wasn't a bit bothered by all the comings and going – or perhaps he didn't notice. How could two cats be so different? Moving day arrived. Buggins stayed on his pile of newspapers in the kitchen, right up to the moment when Molly put him into his travelling basket. Ka started the journey in the cardboard container, which they used when they took her to the vet's, but she didn't like it at all. She made that clear from the start. Topher sat on the back seat with a cat on either side of him. Buggins went to sleep straightaway but Ka started yowling.

'Mi – OW! MI – OW – OW!' It was an affronted – how can you do this to me, Topher? Then she started scratching the cardboard. Then she yowled again.

'MI – OW – OW – OW!' It wasn't long before her claws appeared through the cardboard. Even before they reached the motorway Chris Hope said, 'For heaven's sake, Topher, let her out!'

They all agreed that she would be okay with Topher on the back seat of the car and they were right – up to a point. She quickly settled down on his knee. He picked the shreds of cardboard out of her claws and then she slept, till they stopped at a service station. It was late afternoon by then and quite dark. She woke up when the car stopped and Topher lifted her gently onto the back seat before sliding out of the half open door. When they returned she had gone back to sleep. Topher opened the rear door carefully and wasn't quite sure what happened next.

From out of the darkness a large dog appeared, barking. Before Topher could close the door it had leaped past him and had its forepaws on the back seat. Then its owner shoved past Topher, grabbed the dog's collar and hauled it away. It was too late. The damage was done. Ka had gone, probably out of the driver's door. His dad had been getting in at the time. Immediately they all started searching the car park calling her name. It was difficult to see and desperately worrying because there was a lot of traffic.

Molly said, 'She's most likely hiding in those shrubs.' Gardens bordered the car park. 'Having a pee perhaps.'

But she wasn't digging or squatting in the gardens. They searched for an hour before Topher's dad said they must go. By this time it was very dark, except for the lights in the car park and on the motorway nearby. Traffic thundered along it. Topher begged to stay longer and search, but he wasn't allowed. All he could do was plead with the staff at the café and the petrol station to keep their eyes open. He gave them LOST CAT notices too, but as they drove away he felt sick with worry. He felt even sicker when he found the statue of Ka on the floor of the car.

Chapter 3

When they arrived at Fletcher House he put the statue, which looked dull and lifeless, on his bedside table. Then he made up his bed, which seemed small in his spacious new room. The whole house seemed vast and echoey. The removal men had put down most of the carpets and some furniture, but then they'd left.

Where was Ka? *When* was Ka?

She'd obviously gone time-travelling to escape the dog. After all the recent changes in her life, an unfriendly dog had been the final straw. He longed to be with her. She might need him. He hated his new bedroom – the infantile wallpaper especially. It had the carol, *I saw three ships come sailing by*, all over it. His dad had promised it would be decorated before they moved in. It could have been worse he supposed. At least he liked sailing. But even the thought of sailing didn't cheer him up. He was too worried about Ka.

He was too worried to eat much of the Indian take-away that his dad sent out for. The three of them ate it in their new kitchen. A copper lamp hung over the table, bathing them all in a friendly glow, but no one said much. In the middle of it Chris Hope said, 'For heaven's sake, Topher, try and cheer up. Cats do have nine lives you know.'

Later, back in his bedroom, he wondered if his dad could be right. Righter than he knew. So far, Ka had had two lives – that Topher knew about anyway – the first as a temple cat in Ancient Egypt, the second as a magician's cat in the time of Queen Elizabeth I. What sort of life was she having now?

At nine o'clock he put out the light – at the door because his bedside lamp hadn't been unpacked – intending to have an early night. Ka usually came back in the night. He'd woken up to find it happening – the statue coming to life. Becoming Ka! It was an amazing sight, which he yearned to see again. So he lay in bed staring at the statue, willing it to come to life. But it didn't gleam as it usually did when it was about to come to life. In fact he couldn't see it at all in the darkness. He had to put out his hand to reassure himself that it was there, feel the smooth, cold stone beneath his fingers. His room was too dark, that was part of the problem, even though there were no curtains covering the diamond-shaped panes of glass. Cloud covered the moon and Fletcher House stood well back from the road. A row of fir trees blocked the light from the street lamps.

After a bit, he tried not staring. He tried to get to sleep instead, but just lay there tossing and turning. It was too quiet perhaps – or too noisy – too different anyway and rather cold. He couldn't hear the murmur of his dad and Molly's voices below. They were further away than they had been in Molly's little house. He couldn't hear if they were talking or listening to the radio or television. But he could hear his bedside clock ticking loudly and water gurgling in the central heating pipes. He could hear the house creaking as it started to warm up after weeks of being empty. Reaching out for the statue again, he felt the cold stone beneath his fingers. He felt the shape of Ka's smooth back, sticking-out shoulder blades and long pointed ears. But they were stiff and lifeless. They were stone, just stone. He lifted it slightly and felt the weight in his hand. It felt nothing like Ka. To stop his thoughts getting morbid, he got out of bed, put the light back on and picked up his book about the Romans.

Perhaps she'd gone to see the Romans this time? He hoped so. They liked cats a lot. He studied a photo of a mosaic showing a lovely round-eyed cat holding down a farmyard hen. The Romans kept hens because they loved eating eggs and not just hens' eggs. They sought out new taste sensations. They did make animal sacrifices to their gods it seemed, but not of cats as far as he could tell. They were very superstitious and thought that success in life was all a matter of luck. But they hedged their bets by trying to bribe the gods, especially the goddess Fortuna, Lady Luck herself. If she liked you, you would be rich and prosperous. If she didn't you were doomed.

Eventually he fell asleep and when he woke up it was light and Ka was there on the end of his bed! The statue had gone – and she was there! He felt her before he saw her, heavy on his feet. Hardly daring to believe it, he sat up and there she was curled up, a furry cushion. Fast asleep. He was delighted of course. He was *thrilled* with happiness but couldn't help feeling a bit cheated.

He'd wanted to see it happen – the statue becoming Ka.

'Where has she come from?' His dad, carrying tea and toast, did a double-take in the doorway.

'I don't know.' Topher wished he could have seen her returning.

His dad called out, 'Molly! Look at this!'

And Ka woke up.

Then Molly appeared, bleary-eyed, clutching her dressing gown over her bump as Ka stretched luxuriously into an arch. 'Ka! Where were you hiding? You definitely weren't there when I put Topher's light out, at about half past ten.'

His dad said, 'She must have been hiding somewhere, and in the car too. She must have got out when I put the car in the garage. That really is an amazing animal.'

Ka padded along to Topher and greeted him nose to nose. She seemed to smile. Chris Hope and Molly went back to their room.

Topher said, 'Where have you been, Ka?'

She began to purr.

Rrrr. Rrrr.

'Where have you been?'

But she was more interested in the toast on his plate – or rather the butter. He cut the toast into quarters and let her lick one piece. Sometimes she ate toast but not today.

'Well, you're certainly not starving, Ka. And you seem to be in good condition.' He examined her carefully, parting her fur with a pencil, so he could see the skin beneath. Once she had come back with a wound on her neck. He ate some toast himself, then let her lick his buttery fingers with her rough tongue.

'Tell me, where have you been?'

But she just carried on licking. And he remembered how she usually answered that question. Of course! She spelled it out on his computer! Now where was his computer? Easing himself out of bed carefully, so as not to disturb her, he started to look. Where had the removal people put it? As soon as he got it set up he would ask her again.

Chapter 4

He couldn't find his computer. Molly and his dad couldn't find theirs. Molly rang Packards to complain but had to leave a message on the answer-phone because it was a Sunday. Ka spent the morning walking round the house sniffing and rubbing her cheeks against things. It was 'owning' behaviour and she made sure she owned something in every room. She had done the same when she moved into Molly's little terrace. Now she had lots of rooms to visit. Buggins didn't seem to realise he had moved. He just slept in his box, which Molly had put next to the boiler in the laundry room, which was next to the kitchen. She had also rubbed his paws with butter as soon as they arrived. It wasn't superstition, she said, but good scientific sense. Cats liked butter. She buttered Ka's paws as well and showed her the catmint cutting that she'd brought from the Cambridge house. In summer Ka went mad for catmint, but she only sniffed the plant once, probably because there were only a few tiny leaves to smell. Eventually she settled down on top of the boiler, where she looked down on Buggins.

Topher spent the day unpacking, arranging his room, and not looking forward to school next day. From time to time he asked Ka where she had been, but she wasn't in a talkative mood. When she came upstairs with him at bedtime he asked her again. She was on the middle of his bed going round in circles. As he pulled on his pyjamas, he said, 'Don't go away, Ka. Everything's new and I need you.'

But she just carried on beating the duvet into submission. When at last she settled down, all four paws tucked neatly beneath her, he knelt by the bed for a face to face.

'Where did you go, Ka? Tell me, please.'

She opened her eyes and began to purr.

Rrrr...Rrrr...

'Rome, Ka? Is that what you're saying?'

Possibly. Possibly not.

'If you go away, leave a message, like you did before. So don't go away till I've got my computer back. Right?'

She curled into a ball with her tail over her eyes. He got into bed, carefully, so as not to disturb her. Rain started to drum against the window. He caught sight of his new school uniform, which he'd draped round the room, to try and make it look a bit worn. The blue tie with the golden-eagle crest hung from the door handle. He wasn't looking forward to being a new boy again.

It was still raining when he set off in the morning. As he reached the end of the close where it joined the main road, a school bus drew up and a gang of boys and girls in green uniforms got on. One girl noticed him and called something out – it sounded like snob – but it wasn't long before he was wishing he'd got on it too. His first day at Noviomagus didn't go too well, mostly because one boy in his class seemed to dislike him on sight.

*

When he walked into 7G, a classroom with high-up windows and brown-tiled walls, the teacher was taking the register. Mr Gentry was a pale man with rimless glasses and the class sat in straight lines facing him. Topher didn't notice any individuals – just an assortment of faces – till the teacher told him to take the empty seat by Sanjit. Sanjit was dark with a toothy grin. He sat at the front near the window. He introduced him to the two boys sitting behind and across from him. Matt was freckly. Ollie wore glasses. That was all Topher managed to take in. They seemed friendly which was a relief. After register he tagged along to lessons with them. It was during rugger after break that he noticed Brett Durno – he learned his name later – when the thug punched him during a game of rugger.

At first Topher thought it was an accident or even part of the game. He'd never played rugger before, because he'd always been to soccer-playing schools. He knew it was rough though. He mentioned his lack of experience to the teacher at the start of the lesson, but Mr Welkins, a large hairy Welshman, just said, 'You've seen it on the box, haven't you?' He told him he'd catch on. He put him in a team and told him he was a second row forward. The punch to his ribs during the first ruck came from his own side – he thought – so it was even more of a surprise. He thought he might have been mistaken. But by the end of the game, when it had happened three times, he knew who had punched him and that it was deliberate.

His attacker was of average build with short brownish

hair and blue-grey eyes, Topher noted later. There was nothing to show he was a sadist – except his hard expression. As he passed by on the way to the showers, Topher thought of tackling him about it but didn't, mostly because he didn't know what to say. His ribs were red and hurt a lot, but the boy next to him was boasting about his injury, a kick to the shins. In fact lots of boys were showing off lurid bruises received in previous games. During lunch he managed to find out from Sanjit that his name was Brett Durno. Sanjit said he was an 'okay sort of guy'. But in the next lesson, the okay sort of guy cut Topher, literally. He made it look like an accident, but it wasn't.

It was biology and they were all dissecting onions to see the cell structure. Brett pushed Topher's arm as he passed, on his way to the back of the lab. Nobody else saw what happened, but Sanjit heard Topher gasp and saw the result – a spurt of blood. Then the teacher noticed and rushed over.

'Idiot!' He was a teacher Sanjit had warned him about, during the lunch hour, one of several with a short fuse. 'Didn't I tell you to be careful?' he yelled grabbing Topher's arm and leading him to the cold tap. Fortunately the cut – on the middle finger of his left hand – wasn't deep. The blade had only sliced the skin, but it could have been much worse. Mr Skeet put a plaster on the wound, which stopped bleeding quite quickly. Then he said, 'Right, what happened?'

He had to record all accidents in a book, he said. When Topher told him what had happened, precisely what had happened, the teacher called Brett Durno out and asked him what had happened.

Brett Durno said, 'I was on my way to my place. Next thing I heard the new boy yell.'

'Did you knock him, accidentally I mean?'

'No, sir.'

Mr Skeet let Brett go back to his place then said quietly, 'I thought you were mistaken, boy. Durno isn't that sort. Now go and get on with your work, and be more careful in future.'

Both Sanjit and Ollie said Brett Durno hadn't got a reputation for bullying, or anything like that. He was the quiet sort who didn't say much. Topher asked where he lived, because he was a bit worried about what might happen on the way home, if he lived nearby. They both said they didn't know. Boys came to Noviomagus from all over the area. They didn't say they didn't believe Topher, who had told them what happened, but they both looked a bit wary and slightly less friendly, he thought.

And that afternoon Brett Durno *did* seem to be following him home, or going in the same direction anyway. Glancing back, Topher noticed him about a hundred metres behind him on the main road, but later he went left at the crossroads where Topher turned right. It was a relief, but not a complete relief, because he obviously did live in the same village.

When he got home Molly noticed the plaster straight away. He told her what had happened in the lab and in the rugger lesson. She told his dad who rang the school, after a bit of chivvying from Molly, who said it was best to nip these things in the bud. When Chris Hope came back from the phone, he said the head had promised to look into it, but urged them not to be too hasty in their judgements. Dr Warman said Topher must write down everything that had happened while it was still fresh in his mind. He would read it himself. Meanwhile he would ask his staff to keep an eye on things, discreetly.

Molly said he could use her lap-top to write his report if he wished. His own computer still hadn't arrived. His dad's had and so had Molly's, but his hadn't. Packards were looking for it. It was very annoying. The only good thing was that Ka was still there. She was on the boiler when he came in, but saw that he needed her and followed him upstairs to his room. He sat on his bed and switched on Molly's computer to write down exactly what had happened – and Ka jumped onto his knee. He said, 'Sit beside me please, Ka,' because he could hardly see the screen with her there, but she wouldn't get off. She did settle down though, facing the screen, and he remembered what he wanted to ask her. So with difficulty he typed in the question: WHERE DID YOU GO, KA? And she put out a paw to press the keyboard. The keys were small on the lap top and she seemed to have difficulty pressing only one at a time, but at last something took shape on the screen.

,,,,L XX**IX

What did that mean?

Chapter 5

He thought it might be a number in Roman numerals –
a date perhaps?

He worked it out. 79.

He said, 'You're a clever cat, Ka. That's interesting,
but I'd like to know *where*. Please.'

She purred but her paws were tucked beneath her and
her eyes were closed. He tickled her ear. 'Dozy. I said
where.' He typed the question again: WHERE DID
YOU GO, KA?

And she opened her eyes, untucked her paws and
touched the keyboard again. Again she found it hard to
press the tiny keys one at a time, but letters appeared on
the screen. A word took shape.

CA;;llevA

It took him a few moments to catch on.

'Cal-le-va?' He sounded it out. 'Calleva! You went to
Calleva, Ka? You went to Silchester?' Remembering the
cat's pawprint in the tile, questions rushed into his head.
This was more than interesting. It was exciting. He
longed to know more, but she jumped off his knee and
went downstairs.

He started on the report then, but found it more
difficult than he anticipated. He began to have doubts
about what had happened. When he read through what
he'd written it sounded unlikely. Everyone else thought
Brett Durno was an okay person. What motive did he

have for a start? So he did the report, but he didn't print it out. The printer wasn't fixed up anyway and the urge to nail Brett Durno had subsided. He didn't want people thinking *he* was a troublemaker. Perhaps it would be best to wait and see.

The rest of the week passed slowly. He was lonely in fact, but at least Brett Durno left him alone. Most people left him alone and he hoped he hadn't already put people off. There was no rugger. That was another good thing. The weather was so bad, with rain and mist blowing in from the sea, that all outdoor sport was cancelled. They played five-a-side soccer in the sports hall instead. Brett Durno was sometimes absent, though Topher couldn't be sure of this. So many boys were doing other things, like rehearsing for concerts or quizzes or the school play that the normal time-table was suspended. Most teachers strolled into the classroom, did a count of who was there and told the few who were to get on with something quietly. Sanjit and Ollie were in the school play, which was *Julius Caesar*. They said it was a good laugh and told Topher to get tickets.

On Thursday morning Brett Durno was present. During register, Mr Gentry handed Topher an application form for the Sailing Club. Topher had told him he wanted to join. The teacher told him to fill it in and go to the gym hall at lunchtime. He said, 'Brett will help if you've got any questions, won't you, Brett? He's in the Sailing Club.' Then he left the room. So did quite a few of the boys including Sanjit and Ollie. Topher couldn't see Brett's reaction because he was at the front – Brett

30

sat at the back – but when he was halfway down the form, he realised someone was reading over his shoulder. Resisting the temptation to cover up the form, he finished writing that he was RYA level 3 before looking up – and Brett Durno moved swiftly to the door and out into the corridor. Again, Topher got the impression he'd done something to annoy him.

This was confirmed when he reached the gym at lunchtime. Brett Durno was standing with one foot across the doorway. Inside, at the far end of the gym was a teacher who looked like Captain Birdseye and a group of boys gathered round a television. Brett Durno said, 'I think you've got the wrong room.' He looked at his feet as he spoke. Topher was wondering what to do when the teacher called out, 'Come along, you two! We're going to start.'

Brett moved his foot. Then the two of them walked the length of the hall to a gym mat in front of a TV.

Captain Birdseye's real name was Mr Trustram, but most of the boys called him Skip. He welcomed Topher, whom he seemed to be expecting, and told him they were going to watch a video. It was about some dinghy races called the Frostbite Series, which took place in the Christmas holidays. Topher and Brett watched the video from opposite ends of the gym mat and once he'd seen it Topher was determined to take part. He'd been longing to sail again but thought he'd have to wait till spring. These winter races looked thrilling. Nothing was going to stop him taking part. Certainly not a scab like Brett Durno, who did look scabby round his nose.

Surprisingly, he was a bit of a star in the club, and Mr Trustram asked him to give out application forms for the Frostbite course, saying you had to be at least RYA level 3 to qualify. When Brett ignored his outstretched hand, Topher asked him for one. Mr Trustram was standing nearby when he asked.

He filled in the form that night before setting off for *Julius Caesar* with Molly and his dad. The play was quite good. The school had a proper theatre with tiered seats and they had decent ones about halfway back. Matt and Ollie came on first wearing white togas. They were Roman tribunes, breaking up a crowd of Julius Caesar's supporters who had gathered in the Forum. Then Sanjit came on warning Caesar he was going to be killed. Topher didn't recognise Sanjit at first. He was a sooth-sayer – which was a sort of fortune teller – and he wore a long wig. In the next scene, you realised he was right. Some men *were* planning to murder Caesar and the tension mounted. Sanjit kept wailing, 'Beware the Ides of March! Beware the Ides of March!' But Caesar kept on ignoring him, saying he wasn't superstitious and then suddenly the Ides of March, whatever they were, arrived and Caesar was being killed. His so-called friends were all stabbing him with swords and daggers, and blood was spreading over his white toga.

During the interval Molly and his dad stayed in their seats, because they didn't want coffee, which was being served in the library. That was okay till there was a cry of 'Salutations!' and there was Dr Warman, swooping down on them from the back of the theatre, nose first like a great black eagle. Topher buried his head in the programme and learned that the Ides of March was a date, 15th March, and that the play contrasted two different beliefs – one that Fate ruled your life and the other that destiny was in your own hands, or rather your own character. The Romans tended to be Fatalists. Topher was wondering what he believed when he heard the head saying, 'And young Topher, no more trouble I hope?'

It was a relief when a bell rang and the head went back to his seat. Soon afterwards the lights were dimmed. Topher didn't enjoy the second half as much as the first, partly because no one he knew was in it. He found his mind wandering during some of the longer speeches, and was quite glad when the body of Brutus, the chief conspirator, was carried off, leaving another pool of blood on the stage. The play ended, leaving the impression that the Romans were a bloodthirsty lot. Topher thought about Ka's message. What had she seen on her Roman travels? He looked forward to seeing her when they got home.

They walked back under a starry and moonlit sky. The pavements sparkled with frost and he and his dad held Molly's arms in case she slipped. In the close one house had a Christmas tree in its window. Quite a few had fairy lights on trees in their gardens. Their own house looked warm and welcoming when they walked up the drive. Lots of lights were on. His dad started to complain about electricity bills, but Molly laughed and told him not to spoil a lovely evening. She said having lights on deterred burglars. Ka didn't come to greet them. She didn't seem to be anywhere in the house, but at least the statue wasn't beside his bed. Topher went outside and called her till his dad insisted he went to bed. It was while he sat in bed drinking hot chocolate, that he noticed the writing on the wallpaper beside his bed. It was on the sail of one of the little ships in black felt tip. The writing was small but meant to be seen. BEWARE THE TIDES OF MARCH. But MARCH was crossed out and December was written in its place.

Someone had been in his room. He was certain. Someone who had seen the play had been in his room. It was too much of a coincidence to be otherwise. But this had been done tonight, so the writer must have seen the play yesterday. They'd had burglars despite all the lights being on. But *who* was it and how had they got into his room? For a horrible moment he thought someone might still be there. Might be under the bed or in the wardrobe. It was a scary feeling.

'We've had burglars!' He raced downstairs.

His dad came out of his study shushing. Molly had just gone to bed he said. Topher explained about the writing. His dad looked doubtful but came up to see. He examined it, then opened the wardrobe and looked under the bed – to prove to Topher there was no one there. Then he said the writing must have been there for a while. He pointed to other scribbling on the wallpaper. He said Topher hadn't noticed it earlier, that was all. The wording was a coincidence, he said. They were famous words. Nobody could have got in. The burglar alarm would have gone off. Then Molly appeared in her dressing gown and agreed with him. Topher felt sick. Someone had been in his bedroom. He was sure of it. He felt invaded. It was like the feeling he had when strangers, prospective buyers, had come peering into his bedroom, but much much worse. Molly looked sympathetic. His dad looked impatient. He said again, 'No one has been into the house, Topher. That must have been written by the previous occupant. It's a joke and a coincidence, nothing more. Now let's put our imaginations to bed and get a good night's sleep.'

He thought Topher had imagined it.

'Goodnight, Topher.'

His dad put his arm round Molly.

She said, 'Goodnight, Topher. Don't worry.'

Then they went to their room, leaving him alone

'Ka!' He needed her. Where was she?

Glancing down, he saw her statue half-hidden under his bed. He picked it up and placed it on his bedside table.

Chapter 6

The statue glowed slightly. That was the good thing. When he put out the light and got into bed, it glowed more brightly in a pool of golden light. So he sat watching, willing it to glow more brightly still, to smoulder and burn as some force breathed life into the stone and transformed it into Ka. He longed to see her eyes gleaming, casting circles of light onto the wall opposite. He longed to see the circles moving from left to right and right to left – because that is what had happened before. Determined not to fall asleep and miss it this time, he propped himself against the pillows and prepared himself for a long wait – because it usually happened in the middle of the night when the house was silent and still.

But he could still hear noises from nearby rooms. A newspaper rustled; voices murmured; a door clicked shut; water gurgled; water swooshed down from the tank in the attic. It sounded as if his dad was having a shower. A line of light under the door showed that the landing light was still on. Footsteps. A door click. The light went off. The statue still shone. Hardly daring to move he watched it though his eyelids grew heavy as the house grew quieter, quieter.

Come on, Ka. Come home. He willed her to return.

'*Come home, Ka. I need you*,' he whispered into the darkness, trying to stay awake. But he must have fallen asleep despite his efforts, because later – how much later? – he found himself waking up in total darkness. What time was it? Why had he woken up? For a moment he forgot the statue and groped in the darkness for the lamp switch and his bedside clock. He reached out but couldn't feel them. Remembering then that he had moved and was in a strange house, he tried to orientate himself and suddenly saw books on his bookshelf, their titles spotlighted by twin spotlights moving from left to right! Right to left! *Then* he remembered the statue, and realising that he had turned away from it in his sleep he turned back.

The statue was glowing brightly.

It was smouldering, its eyes gleaming!

It was becoming brighter by the second. Its eyes were blazing, its surface shimmering, rippling, swelling, fluffing out tuft by tuft, becoming Ka! Becoming fluffy Ka! Suddenly her mouth opened, a diamond of pink.

'Mwa!' *Touch me, Topher*!

He reached out and touched the fur between her ears.
'Ka!'

'*Tophe...rrr*,' she purred ecstatically.

He stroked her head and her fluffy honey-gold fur flecked with black and white settled sleekly.

'*Rrr...rrr...*' Her fluffy tail smoothed. Her body fur became velvet soft and the ankh in the centre of her forehead shone glossy and black. Then the tip of her nose turned pink.

'Ka! I'm so glad you're back.'

White whiskers sprang from her face.

'Mwa!'

Her voice came from the darkness now. He could see only her eyes shining, amber rings circling black pupils. He switched on his bedside lamp and there she was, shining again, but as a real, live, healthy cat shines. In the light of the lamp her pupils shrank to flecks of black in amber spheres.

'Mwa – wa!'

She seemed happy and hungry.

'Mwa – waa!' She sprang from the table onto the floor and made her way towards the door, plume-tail quivering at the tip.

Downstairs in the kitchen he went to open a tin of Whiskas, but she didn't jump onto the surface to nudge his hand as she usually did, and urge him to go faster.

'Mwa – aa!' She called him over to the fridge where she was rubbing her cheeks against the door.

'You're thirsty then, not hungry? Where have you been? What have you been eating?'

He longed to know but she didn't reply and he filled her dish with the creamy milk they bought specially for her – she didn't like the healthy half-fat stuff – and she lapped it up messily, splashing the tiled floor beneath her dish. Then she was on the move again, leading the way upstairs, back to his bedroom, where she sprang onto his bed.

'Mwa – aa!' He lifted the duvet and she disappeared into the dark cave. Then he got in, curling his body round hers. As he turned out the light he caught sight of the writing on the little sail. BEWARE THE TIDES OF DECEMBER.

What did it mean? Who had written it?

Who had been in his room? The bad feeling came back.

Don't wo...rrry.

Don't wo...rrry. Ka's purrs reassured him. She was back. He could feel her warm fur against his stomach. Tomorrow he would solve the mystery of the message.

Chapter 7

Someone must have a key! He woke up with the answer or half the answer in his head. Who had a key? The estate agent? Of course. Or the previous owners? They might have kept one. Where had they gone? The house had been empty so they had never met. The previous owners had moved out some time before. So they must find out who they were. He rushed into Molly and his dad's room, leaving Ka sleeping.

'We've got to change the locks!'

That was the most important thing, stop them getting in again. It was a horrible feeling knowing strangers could invade your territory. But neither Molly nor his dad was welcoming. His dad spoke from under the bedclothes.

'What is it, Topher? The alarm hasn't gone off yet.'

The bedside clock showed it wasn't yet six.

'I've realised how they got in! Whoever wrote on my wall! They didn't break in, so they must have had a key. So it was probably the previous owners, or the estate agent. He had a key! And a key to the burglar alarm.'

Emerging from under the bedclothes with a groan, his dad suggested that Topher go downstairs and make tea for all of them, while he and Molly thought about it. By this time Molly was awake and Ka had appeared. She followed Topher downstairs demanding to be fed. When he got back with a tray of tea and biscuits his dad said, 'Topher, are you seriously suggesting that we change all the locks in the house? Because you *think* someone has written on your wall. It would cost a fortune.'

'I thought we had plenty of money now.'

'Topher, we are *better off* now. We've been able to buy a really nice house, but the upkeep is going to cost quite a lot – you've seen the size of that boiler – and there's soon going to be an extra mouth to feed.'

He patted Molly's bump, which was big enough now for her to balance a plate on. She smiled at Topher, sympathetically, he thought, but he didn't want sympathy. He wanted action. He couldn't bear it when his dad didn't believe him.

'Do you think I'm lying?'

His dad did at least look embarrassed.

'Topher, I think you're mistaken. That writing could have been there for ages. You've only just noticed it. That is the more likely explanation.'

Topher shook his head.

Molly, always the peacemaker, said, 'We could perhaps find out the name of the previous owners.'

She explained that they had bought the house from the building society, who had repossessed it because the previous owners had got behind with their mortgage payments. She thought she remembered the estate agent saying it was a woman and her son. The father who owned the house had left them.

'Then the building society threw them out? Poor things. They wouldn't be happy about that, would they? I mean, they wouldn't like the thought of new people living in their house.'

He almost felt sorry for the invader.

'Yes. That's what happens if you don't pay the mortgage each month,' said his dad, getting out of bed. 'If you lose your job for instance and can't pay. So I'd better get to work.'

'And me,' said Molly, 'but it might be a good idea to change the main locks,' she added. 'As a precaution.'

'Okay,' Chris Hope said. 'If you insist. But I still think Topher's got an overactive imagination. It's not our fault that the building society threw the previous occupants out. Why should anyone want to attack us?'

Later, as Topher left for school he told Ka – who was sitting on the boiler – that he'd be back at lunchtime, and then he would be off for four weeks. One good thing about Noviomagus School was that the holidays were longer.

The Friday morning at school passed painlessly, better than that in fact. There was a mood of celebration. Brett Durno was there in his usual seat at the back of the class, but he and Topher didn't come into contact. They nearly did though on the way home. It was a bit odd. When he saw Brett walking in front of him with another Noviomagus boy, Topher kept as close as he dared. During the wet weather Molly had dropped him off at school each day, so he still hadn't managed to find out exactly where Brett lived – and he wanted to know. It must be in the same village or beyond it because he'd seen him heading this way before. Fortunately the two boys didn't seem to notice they were being followed. Topher thought Brett Durno would go left at the crossroads as he had on Topher's first day – and he planned to follow him this time – but he didn't go left. The other boy did, but Brett Durno went straight on – for a bit – but then stopped, had a good look round and started walking back in the direction he'd come from. Instinctively Topher stepped to one side where there was a newsagent's set back from the road. A few seconds later, well hidden by a rack of newspapers, he saw Brett Durno walking back the same way he had come. Why? Was he looking for him? He was walking quite fast. When Topher thought it was safe he came out of hiding and looked up the road. The boy had reached the school gates. He must have forgotten something, Topher thought, but then saw him carry on walking to a bus stop. A few minutes later he got on the Chichester bus.

Next day, Saturday, Topher saw him again or thought he did. The circumstances were even odder. They – Topher, his dad and Molly – were in the Arno Centre, a shopping mall, in the town. They'd parked their car at the top and were walking down a spiral slope to the ground floor, when he came to a sudden halt. There was a gang of youths at the bottom smoking, though there were NO SMOKING notices all around and *Brett Durno was with them*, sitting on the mosaic floor with his back against Etam's window. Most shoppers were keeping well away from the gang who looked a bit threatening with their studded jackets and shaved heads, but Topher couldn't help staring. He had to be sure. And suddenly the Brett Durno lookalike saw him staring and turned away to study the dresses in the window, as Topher felt his arm being yanked out of its socket by his dad. Pulling him into the entrance of Boots, he muttered, 'It doesn't do to stare at that type. No wonder you get yourself into trouble.'

Topher's explanation didn't go down well. His dad said the sort of boy who went to Noviomagus School wouldn't mix with the crowd they'd just seen.

On Monday, when Topher was in the house on his own because both Molly and his dad had gone to work, he couldn't help feeling nervous. He still thought someone had a key to the house. He now thought it could be Brett Durno. Perhaps Brett Durno used to live here and that's why he hated him. Perhaps Brett Durno had been pretending to other boys at school that he still lived here? For the first time ever he wished he was back at school, the Noviomagus School. He should have made a more determined effort to find his address. He could even have looked in the register. Fortunately Ka stayed close.

'Am I being stupid?' he asked her as he stacked the breakfast dishes into the dishwasher. She carried on licking the gravy off last night's plates.

'Ought I to be scared? Has he really got it in for me?'

She looked up with serious round eyes.

He decided to spend the morning making models and settled at the kitchen table with some things he'd bought the day before. They'd been to Fishbourne to see the Roman Palace of Cogidubnus, and it had been really good. He'd bought a model kit for a Roman galleon and a mosaic kit, a real one with stones with which he was going to cover a table top, to his own design though, not the one the manufacturers suggested. Ka had given him an idea.

'What shall I do, Ka, the galleon or the mosaic?'

'Mee – w!' She jumped onto the table in front of him and pressed her pink nose against his.

He laughed. Sometimes she seemed to read his mind. His idea was to make a mosaic picture of Ka!

'Okay. I'll do the table first – with you on it.'

He went upstairs for the table.

It was while he was coming downstairs that the phone in the hall rang. He couldn't rush to answer it, but did manage to get there before it stopped ringing. But when he answered the line went dead.

He hung around in the hall for a few minutes, but then went into the kitchen. There was a phone there anyway. Ka was on the window-sill, looking out at the birds in the garden. It was a beautiful garden, even in the winter. A willow dangled its branches into the pond in the middle of the lawn, and there were lots of other trees. He'd hung some food containers on a cherry tree near the house and some acrobatic bluetits were feeding from them. So were some ambitious sparrows who tried to copy their acrobatics. Ka was fascinated by them and a bit offended. She sat snickering at them and Topher decided to sketch her while she was relatively still, for his mosaic picture. But as he picked up his pencil the phone rang again. He picked up the receiver and it went dead again. The same thing happened about half an hour later – and this time he heard someone laughing at the other end.

Nervous wasn't the word for what he felt.

When Molly got in at lunchtime he told her about it. Immediately she rang 1471, and he thought – why didn't I think of that? But when Molly put down the phone she said it had been a caller-didn't-leave-their-number call. Then she rang a locksmith, a Mr Keys whose number she got from the Yellow Pages. He came round later that afternoon to look at what needed to be done and said he'd get new locks fixed by the end of the week. Next day when his dad and Molly went to work Topher put the answer-phone on. When he listened to it at lunchtime there were three messages, one from Molly asking if he was okay, one from Ellie inviting him to stay after Christmas and one from the Truth Sayer. That's what he called himself, the person who whispered, 'Beware the Tides of December!'

Chapter 8

Did Brett Durno want to kill him? Put like that, it sounded stupid. And yet – he remembered his face as he'd walked into the Sailing Club meeting. Brett Durno didn't want him to join the Sailing Club. Brett Durno didn't want him to take part in the Frostbite Series. Brett Durno didn't want him to live here.

He looked for something to do to stop himself feeling nervous. For now he felt eyes peering at him through the windows, heard footsteps on the gravel, saw doors opening. It was hard to concentrate on anything else. The beans on toast he'd made for lunch went cold.

Brett Durno must have a key.

He must have lived here before.

His family must have been turned out. So he'd gone to live somewhere else and got in with the Arno Centre gang. Remembering there was a chain on the front door, he went to fix it and picked up a local newspaper from the hall floor. The headline ARNO CENTRE MENACE caught his eye. The photo wasn't clear enough for him to recognise anyone but the scenario was familiar. A gang of skinheads was making a habit of sniffing glue and hanging round the shopping centre. The gang did a bit of shop-lifting and sometimes threatened people. Inside the paper there was a *How To Tell if your Child is a Glue-Sniffer* article. One of the signs was spots round the mouth and nose. Another was acting out of character. It started to make a sick sort of sense.

Topher went back to the kitchen where Ka was sleeping now, curled up on the kitchen table beneath the pull-down lamp. He put his face against her warm fur and sniffed her new-bread smell. Then, after scanning the back garden through the conservatory windows, and the front garden through the hall window, he went upstairs to fetch the Roman galleon kit.

'Have you ever been on one of these, Ka?'

He imagined her on the deck of the galleon, basking under the hot Mediterranean sun.

'Did you come to Britain on a boat like this?'

He imagined the wind rippling her golden fur and filling the galleon's rust-red sails.

Don't wo...rry. Don't wo...rry. She purred on.

So he cut and stuck and tried to concentrate on the task in hand. The phone didn't ring, thank goodness. He kept the answer-phone on anyway, but didn't hear the echoey voice of anyone leaving a message. Then at four o'clock, when he thought Ellie would be home from school, he returned her call.

'What took you so long?' she wailed. She had been there all day she said, on her own, because the teachers were having a training day. She couldn't believe it when he said he'd already broken up for Christmas.

'It's not fair! You've got a whole week extra!'

When he said that Noviomagus wasn't great, she was a bit more sympathetic.

'What's wrong with it?' she asked. 'Are they all terrible snobs?'

48

He told her about Brett Durno. It was a relief pouring it all out, and even before he'd finished she said, 'It sounds awful. What are you going to do about it? You've got to do something. Report him.'

'Who to?'

'The school. The police. This Mr Trustram, the sailing chap. They've got to know this Brett is a real Jekyll and Hyde. Threatening people – it's against the law!'

Topher said, 'But I haven't got proof it's him.'

She said, 'By the time you've got proof you might be dead. You've got every right to go on that sailing course, Frostbite Series or whatever you call it. Get moving, Topher. Do something.'

He had six days to do something. The course started the following Monday.

When Molly and his dad got back he played the message back to them, and he showed them the newspaper article. Chris Hope still said someone was larking around. Topher said he thought it was Brett Durno, who had had it in for him right from the start. Molly said it was odd that the message on the phone had been the same message as the one on the wallpaper, and that it might be more serious. Whoever it was was persistent. His dad said he would get in touch with Mr Trustram before the course started, tell him about the threats and express their concern that someone might have harmful intentions towards Topher. The teacher would be on the lookout for trouble then. He told Topher not to panic. Molly rang the estate agents who said the previous occupants had been called McPherson, but that didn't prove anything. Some kids had parents or step-parents with different names these days.

The rest of the week passed without much happening. On Friday Mr Keys came round to fix new locks to all the outer doors. On Saturday when they were in the shopping centre again – buying a dry-suit that Topher had to have for the Frostbite course – there was no sign of the gang, but there were a lot of uniformed security guards.

On Sunday night, the night before the course began. Topher went to bed early. Ka came up too, but he couldn't get to sleep. In the end he switched the light back on and read *Swallows and Amazons*. His gran had sent him the book when she heard he had taken up sailing. It was an old-fashioned adventure story set in the Lake District where she lived. It was full of realistic detail about boats and sailing, but seemed like a fantasy, another world in fact. The children took off for whole days in sailing boats, without any adults, and they played at being pirates. They pretended they had dangerous enemies and swore they'd rather drown than be 'duffers'. Duffers were cowards, and Topher decided he was one. Unlike the incredibly named Titty, he'd rather be a duffer than drown. He decided not to go on the course. But by the time he fell asleep he'd changed his mind again. Why should Brett Durno win? Why shouldn't he go on the course? His dad had spoken to Mr Trustram so the teacher would be keeping an eye on things. Brett Durno just wanted to stop him going. He wouldn't actually try to harm him while people were watching. And his unlikely looking friends wouldn't be there egging him on. But next morning, driving to the Marina with his dad, his fears mounted again. It would be quite easy to stage an 'accident' in a boat. Brett Durno was clever and nasty enough to try.

Chapter 9

They were the first to arrive. The Marina car park was empty, the buildings locked and uninviting. The water in the harbour looked calm and sparkled for a few seconds when the winter sun broke through grey cloud, but then became grey and leaden. Dinghies moored at the edge hardly moved.

'See, like a millpond,' his dad said, getting out of the car.

Mr Trustram pulled up beside them in his car.

Feeling sick, Topher stayed inside. You could drown in a millpond as well as anywhere else. You could drown in a puddle. Mr Trustram was shaking hands with his dad now. Suddenly Topher realised his feelings weren't even mixed. He wasn't a hero. He was into survival. He'd rather be a duffer than die – and he'd say so.

Opening the car door a bit, he heard Mr Trustram say, 'And Durno, Brett, he's a good cove. Here he is. Come over here, Brett!'

Then Brett Durno was walking past the half-open door in a tracksuit, looking fit and healthy. No spots that Topher could see. Closing the door again, he saw his dad shaking hands with his enemy. Then more cars pulled up, and more boys and a few girls spilled out of them carrying bulky bags of equipment. Chris Hope returned to the car.

'Topher,' he said confidently, 'I really don't think you

have anything to worry about. It all seems very well organised. Trustram seems well aware of safety issues and he says Brett Durno is a decent sort, I think so too.'

Checking that Topher had his lunch and enough money for the bus fare home – the course finished at three – he started the car engine. Topher got out.

He saw a lot of the 'decent' Durno during the morning, because Mr Trustram got him to demonstrate several techniques before they all practised them. He was obviously a bit of a star in the club and didn't intend to be eclipsed by Topher or anyone else. Standing on the side watching him rig the dinghy, Topher tried to equate the figure before him – a bit of a show-off but competent and good-humoured – with the thug who had punched and cut him, the threatening voice on the phone, the person who had broken into his house. Could sniffing glue really bring about such a character change? Jekyll and Hyde, Ellie had called him, and Hyde – or was it Jekyll? – still seemed reluctant to meet his eye. And at twelve o'clock when they went to eat their packed lunches in the clubhouse, Topher saw him come in the door, note where he, Topher, was sitting, then go to the opposite end.

Fine, Topher thought. That suits me fine.

But the afternoon brought more problems. As soon as they got outside again, Mr Trustram put them all in pairs. Assigning two people to each dinghy he said, 'Topher, you'll crew for Brett, yes, in the *Wayfarer*.' It wasn't a question and he went on, 'You two can show us how to tack.'

They all turned towards the sea for a moment where the tide was going out. As he clambered aboard the dinghy from the pontoon Topher felt nervous again. Nervous wasn't the word. Sitting beside Brett, whose hand was on the tiller he felt scared, not because the water was choppy, though it was – a wind had got up and it suddenly felt much colder – but because the hand on the tiller could easily cause the boat to jibe. It would be so easy to stage an accident. He could be knocked senseless with the boom. All it needed was a sneaky tug of the tiller and he'd be overboard. The grey waters would open and close. He'd be gone. Nobody would know it wasn't an accident.

The tension didn't help his co-ordination. Half expecting some dirty tactics as Brett steered the dinghy towards the southern end of the harbour, Topher tried to keep his wits about him. But his own movements seemed slow and clumsy and the craft didn't respond as it should do. It didn't seem to know in which direction it was going and he felt it was his fault – not the tide and wind working against each other, which was causing the choppiness. Hanging out over the swirling wake, he leaned one way and then the other, responding as fast as he could to Brett's orders, but it was even harder work than usual and the dinghy seemed to resist him. Glimpsing Brett's face, he sensed his scorn and then suddenly things changed.

For a second he felt relief at the calmness of the water. His own movements seemed smoother and he felt more confident, but then he realised that the wind had changed direction, that the big balloon sail was billowing and the helm was high. In fact tide and wind had combined forces to carry them towards the sea! Rapidly he became aware of a strong pull above and below and through him as the craft *streaked* through the water – towards the mouth of the river. As the wind tried to uproot his hair he realised that tide and wind were swooshing them at terrifying speed towards the open sea! He tried not to panic but the waves were getting bigger, the current faster. The open sea was getting closer by the second.

If Brett had engineered this he was already regretting it. There was panic in his voice as he yelled the order. 'Haul on the main and jib sheets!'

Then again. 'Haul in on the main and jib! We'll have to tack back!'

But sailing back against wind and tide was notoriously difficult. Some found it impossible. Desperately, Topher hauled on both ropes. Hung on with all his strength and it seemed to make no difference. Still they were heading for the open sea. Still Topher hung on as Brett tried to steer the tiller. But their efforts seemed useless against the combined force of the wind and tide.

'Haul! Haul!' Brett screeched and Topher hung on as the wind swept through him. Then as a rushing sound filled his ears he thought their efforts might be paying off. Slowly, slowly he realised they were managing to turn the boat to face the wind. So far so good, but no time for rejoicing. There was a long way to go. They were going to have to do the manoeuvre again and again, zig-zagging their way up the estuary.

Freezing spray stung his face.

Rushing wind filled his ears.

'Ready about!' Brett put the tiller across the helm.

'Lee ho!' he yelled, warning Topher that the boom was coming across.

Topher let off the sheets on the port side and hauled in on the other.

'Ready about!' Brett yelled again.

'Lee ho!'

'Ready about!'

'Lee ho!'

Again and again Topher let off the sheets then hauled them in, each time using all his energy, all his concentration, each time knowing he'd have to use it all again and again, a score of times before they reached safety.

'Ready about!' screamed Brett, his voice rising above the screeching wind.

'Lee ho!'

Topher let off the sheets as fast as he could, hauled them in as fast as he could, leaning this way then that, co-ordinating his movements with Brett's, both of them hanging out over the racing water, hoping desperately that they were moving forward against the wind and tide.

And slowly, slowly with tremendous effort they did progress up the harbour, making their way from one side to the other, zig-zagging against the wind and tide. And eventually, eventually – it seemed like days later – they reached the shore to the sound of sirens as the lifeboat crew arrived.

Willing hands helped them onto dry ground.

'Well done, lads. Excellent teamwork,' said Mr Trustram whose normally tanned face was like a stretched sail. 'Brilliant demonstrations of what to do in an emergency. You couldn't have known the wind was going to change like that – none of us did – and you responded in exactly the right way. Both of you. Go and get changed now, then I expect you could do with a hot drink.'

Too exhausted to say anything, Topher went to one end of the changing room Brett to the other. Obviously. They'd left their things at opposite ends. But had anything changed? Topher sensed unspoken thoughts from Brett but couldn't guess what they were. He was sure though that Brett hadn't engineered that danger. That was one good thing. He couldn't have staged that. He couldn't have made the wind change. Nor could he have expected it. And he'd been as scared as Topher was, terrified in fact, and just as relieved when they survived the ordeal. Together. When their lives had been saved – by their own efforts. By their *combined* efforts. They couldn't have done it alone. They'd saved their own lives and they'd saved each other's. They'd helped each other. Deep in thought Topher didn't notice Brett coming towards him, but suddenly became aware that he was standing near, when he thrust out a hand.

'Thanks, mate.'

Topher took it and their eyes met for a second.

Brett's looked as if he might cry.

'I'm...It's...'

But then he'd gone, unable to say what he seemed to want to say, before Topher had time to say anything back. Soon after that several others came into the changing room uttering congratulations. It was a bit embarrassing. Topher didn't stop for a hot drink. He thought he might manage to catch an earlier bus if he set off straightaway. It would save him an hour's wait and he'd be on his way at least, before it was dark. It was getting dark already. The shortest day of the year was fast approaching. Most kids were waiting for their parents to pick them up in cars and when one of them, a boy called Tyro, offered him a lift to the bus station Topher accepted. He thought – hoped – Brett might be going there too, because he'd arrived on foot, but he wasn't around to be asked.

The bus station was a long low building with a covered bit in the middle leading to the bus bays. It was at the end of this, while he was working out which bay his bus would go from, that he saw the gang, obviously the Bus Station gang now. They were near a photo machine and didn't see him. At least he hoped they didn't. He didn't stand and stare for long, just long enough to see that Brett wasn't with them. In fact the bus Topher wanted, a white double-decker, was in so he made his way to it. It was 3.45 exactly when he sat down near the middle of the lower deck and the bus shuddered to life. The lights flickered – it was getting dark outside – and the doors started to close with a hiss. Then opened again as one by one the gang climbed aboard.

Topher slumped down in his seat but they saw him, he

was sure of it. Perhaps they had seen him earlier. And if he had any doubts who they were, their smell, a mixture of ash and glue, dispelled them. They paid for their tickets and went upstairs. Unable to hear what stop they asked for, he hoped they would get out before he did. The bus was one of those that went round half the town putting people down at every stop, before it headed out for the villages. Hardly anyone else got on, so by the time it left the town Topher was the only one downstairs – except the driver of course – and the gang. They didn't get out. They were quiet but he felt scared. Somehow he knew they had it in for him.

He tried giving himself reasons not to be scared, that he and Brett Durno were no longer enemies for one. He felt sure that something had been resolved between them. Brett had been trying to explain and apologise. But the upstairs lot didn't know that and maybe Brett wasn't part of their gang now.

His thoughts stopped when he saw a shaved head with snakes tattooed all over it, hanging upside down from the stairway. Then it withdrew to a burst of laughter. Another head took its place, one with a ring in its lip. The smell of glue was stronger now, the laughter louder. Had they got glue up there? The bus passed the newsagent's where he'd hidden once to watch Brett walk past – it seemed a long time ago – and a neon light shone out of the darkness. The bus driver looked uneasy. Would the thugs get off at the next stop? He hoped not because it was his stop too. Then he saw red traffic lights ahead and he was on his feet asking the driver if he could get off. And the driver, muttering that it was against the law, seemed to understand.

The doors hissed open.

Topher got off.

Then he ran.

Faster than he'd ever run before.

He couldn't remember crossing the road, or checking for traffic.

He couldn't remember feeling for his key in his pocket, but he had it in his hand as he reached the front door, which opened instantly. He fell inside and slammed it shut with his feet. Then he lay on the floor for several minutes waiting for his breathing to return to normal. But before it did he heard feet crunching up the drive. He heard someone trying a key in the lock.

Chapter 10

The door didn't open. They had the wrong key –
fortunately. Thank God the locks had been changed. But
they were angry – that was bad. It sounded as if they
were trying to kick the door in. They were shouting too.
Swearing mostly.

'Open up or we'll kick the door in!' That was clear
enough.

'It's not your house anyway!'

'It's Bretto's house!'

'You turned him out!'

He'd guessed right.

'Poor ol' Bretto!'

'You bastard!' Something thudded against the door.
Thank God it was solid oak. Suddenly everything made
a horrible sort of sense.

'It's not my fault. We're friends now.' The words he
spoke to himself sounded pathetic and useless. The yobs
at the door were in no mood to listen anyway. They
sounded like maniacs.

'Are you gonna let us in?' Topher, still full length on
the floor, saw the letterbox click open and a steel ring in
a top lip.

He didn't answer. Couldn't answer. All his effort went
into thinking clearly. He must get help. Ring the police,
that was it. He started to creep towards the phone on the
other side of the hall as the letterbox snapped shut and

the window at the side shattered. Then he saw a gloved hand feeling for the lock. It couldn't reach, thank God. He reached for the phone as the hand retreated. But then as he dialled 999 the hand appeared again holding a knife.

The blade was a good four inches long.

'We'll get you, you bastard.'

A woman's voice said, 'Emergency services. Which do you require? Fire, Ambulance or Police?'

As quickly and clearly as he could, he explained the situation.

'Address?'

He gave it.

'Help will be with you in approximately ten minutes.'

'*Ten minutes!*'

'Stay calm,' the voice continued. 'The police and fire service are on their way. Are the intruders still there?'

'I don't know.'

The knife had gone and it was quiet outside, but ominously quiet. He hadn't heard footsteps going away. Hadn't heard them crunching down the gravel drive. So they were probably still out there, in the darkness waiting. Or they might be looking for another way in.

'Where are your parents?' The voice on the phone was kind and calm.

He told her where they worked and said they should be home by now.

'Would you like me to try and contact them?'

'Yes.' Why weren't they home already? With fumbling fingers, he flicked though the phone book and

62

gave her their numbers and their mobile phone numbers.

She said she would get a colleague to ring them.

Then he heard the sound of glass breaking. Upstairs.

Suddenly he remembered Ka who often slept on his bed. Where was she? Why hadn't he seen her? Why hadn't she appeared as she usually did? More glass broke. Surely that would wake Ka? He glanced up the stairs, expecting to see her streaking down. Nothing. Then he heard a wail of distress.

'Mwaa!'

She must be petrified. *Petrified?* Oh no!

He was up the stairs in seconds and there she was on the landing floor, a stone cat on her side near a heap of broken glass. He crouched to examine her. Not her, it. Ka herself was somewhere else and he longed to be with her. An icy wind blew in, whipping the curtains.

'Hello. Hello. Topher Hope. Are you still there?' Below in the hall the phone dangled.

'Hello, Topher, are you still there?' another voice sneered.

It was Ring-lip, peering in through the broken window. About to step inside he held a knife in his gloved hand. Now, as a four-inch blade glinted for a second in the light from the landing, Topher remembered Mr Keys saying that the porch below the window was a security risk. Fearing for his life, he saw Ring-lip turn slightly as something outside shrieked. A look of horror froze the yob's profile. He stared open-mouthed. And Topher stared too – at a huge bird which was lunging at the yob with outstretched wings and hooked beak.

'Eeeek! Eeeek!'

Golden wings, each a metre wide, beat slowly, making a loud rhythmic swishing sound. Golden eyes stared at Ring-lip who wobbled slowly, then fell slowly off the porch.

Down down down.

Topher felt as if he was watching a slow-motion film, as if he was looking at a huge screen. But he wasn't. He was part of what was happening. As Ring-lip disappeared into the darkness below the bird, a golden eagle came closer closer closer filling the window with its swishing wings, till it landed on the porch roof. Then Topher could see its huge four-toed feet, covered with horny scales, could see claws like iron hooks. Could see round golden eyes and a curved cleaver beak, which for a second reminded him of Dr Warman.

'Eee, eee,' said the bird, turning so its tail feathers were facing Topher, who knew what was happening, knew what he must do, for he had done it before.

'Eeek, eeek.'

He climbed onto the window-sill, stepping carefully over the jagged glass onto the porch roof. And then he clambered up the springy tail feathers, clinging to the laterals which parted only slightly as he pulled himself up and up, till at last he reached the top, and then, as the bird raised its tail, he felt himself falling towards the hollow of its back. Then he was landing breathless, in a kneeling position, with his arms round the bird's strong neck.

Spread out below the garden glistened. The drive was a frozen river, the plumed pampas grass in the middle of the lawn a sparkling fountain. Every tree was a glittering Christmas tree in the light of the winter moon. By the gatepost three figures clung together trembling with fear and cold, hallucinating, they thought, like never before. Staring up with glassy eyes they couldn't quite believe what was happening above them. They'd forgotten Ring-lip, motionless on the ground beneath the porch.

Topher raised a hand to wave, then felt the bird moving beneath him, felt himself rocking slightly as the majestic bird, the imperial eagle, the king of birds stepped towards the edge of the porch. As it moved its head from left to right, right to left, searching the landscape and taking bearings he caught glimpses of its black-rimmed golden eyes and wondered which direction it would take.

Where were they going to?

When were they going to?

Clinging now with both arms, he felt the bird tense beneath him, saw its huge wings sink then rise, and they were off! On either side of him the wings rose and fell, effortlessly it seemed, filling his ears with sound, and he saw Fletcher House beneath him, then Noviomagus School, then the town with the market cross in the centre of the chequerboard of roads. But as the bird speeded up landmarks appeared for seconds only and were soon a blur, as the bird moved through the air at amazing speed and they left the earth's surface. Soon they were passing balls of fire – stars close-up! – and balls of fire with tails passed them and some exploded. And then the bird was soaring on still, silent wings through velvety darkness and Topher was thrilled with the wonder of it. Thrilled to be travelling back through time. Thrilled because he wasn't afraid this time, didn't worry that he might become a baby, or an egg or nothing at all. Thrilled because he knew that he was leaving the Earth's surface to re-enter it at another time. Thrilled, most of all, because he was going to be re-united with Ka!

Whoosh! Whoosh! As the wings began to move again, Topher wondered who he would be this time. Three thousand years ago he'd been an Egyptian boy and Ka had been a temple cat. Three hundred years ago he had been an Elizabethan boy who had sailed with Sir Francis Drake, and Ka had been a magician's cat.

Where was he going now?

Was Ka there already?

Who was he going to be?

Now as the bird's wings beat rhythmically beside him his eyelids felt heavy. Up and down. Up and down, their movement lulled and mesmerised him. Up and down, up and down, he had to close his eyes, had to rest his head on the ruff of feathers round the bird's broad neck.

Then he slept.

When he woke up, he thought he was passing through cloud, thought he was entering the Earth's atmosphere again, but that must have happened some time ago. He was on Earth now, on *earth*. He could feel grass under his knees, see movement through a grey mist. There was a drumming in his ears.

Chapter 11

Drums beat. War horns bellowed.

War horses pawed the ground. It was about to begin –
the battle he had been waiting for. It was early morning.
Soon chariots would charge and the clash of iron blades
would ring out through the mist. Crouching in the long
grass in front of the stockade, Topher felt his pulses
racing. How he longed to be down there on the plain.
How he yearned to be in the thick of the fighting,
hacking away at the foe like Bryn his father and Bryn his
brother. If only he were old enough to fight the enemies
of his tribe – or even get close enough to see them
clearly. But his father had ordered him to watch the
battle from the ramparts, from behind the stockade in
fact, but it was hard enough to see even in front of it.

'You could be useful,' Bryn the Elder had said. 'Keep
a look out for fire-raisers sneaking up the side of the
enclosure. And learn what you can for the day you will
have to fight. There'll be more battles. With neighbours
like ours, to be an Atrebatan is to be a warrior, though
we would rather farm and live in peace.'

He didn't mention the Romans but Topher knew he
dreamed of fighting them too, driving them back to
where they'd come from. But the Romans were cleverer
than the British tribes. They didn't attack directly, not
often anyway, though they had a deadly army. They
preferred to take over by stealth, had been doing so for

years. There were more straight-sided Roman buildings in the stronghold now than good round British ones, and more straight Roman roads, built by British slaves! The slaves had been first to throw in their lot with the foreigners. Roman masters were fairer than the British, they said. But it wasn't just slaves who had no honour. Some highborn women married Romans now, wore Roman clothes and Roman jewellery, used their eating pots and called the settlement by its Roman name. Calleva! Topher found it hard to say the word. He hated the Romans. Before they came he had been a proper chieftain's son, though a younger one, and people looked up to him. Now more than half the tribe treated the Romans as masters.

But now it was a neighbouring tribe, the Catuvellauni causing trouble, making another attempt to take over the stronghold. Fortunately the Atrebates were ready for them. Topher thought of his mother and sisters safe inside the stockade as he peered into the mist. It would be disastrous if an enemy did manage to creep up and throw a flaming torch over the stockade onto a thatched roof. If only the mist would clear. Perhaps it was clearing. In the east the sky was lightening.

Then drum beats quickened.

War horns bellowed more loudly and his heart beat faster. Any moment now his father would give the order for his brightly painted warriors to charge. Then battle would begin. Pushing back his long fair hair, Topher tried to make out what was happening. He still couldn't see the Catuvellauni but could just make out the shape of the Atrebatan troops. In the front was a line of horse-drawn chariots, behind them several rows of foot-fighters and suddenly – as sun broke through the cloud – he felt a surge of pride as he saw his father in the middle chariot, legs astride, spear in one hand shield in the other, arms and torso decorated with swirling patterns of brilliant blue. His golden hair spiked like rays of sun crowned his noble head! What a sight!

'Wallooh!' With a wild battle cry, Bryn the Elder's chariot hurtled forward! So did Bryn the Younger's. They were off!

'Wallooh! Wallooh!'

Father and son hurtled forwards, just two in a wave of chariots, raising clouds of rolling dust, which hid the fighting men behind them, and the enemy in front of them. Beneath Topher the earth trembled. What was happening? He wished he knew but all he could see was dust. Where were the Catuvellauni? He still hadn't seen them. Had the sight of armed Atrebatans put them to flight already? Had the mere sight of his father at the head of his troops filled them with fear? No wonder. For several minutes as he strained to see, Topher's hopes rose. But then – as the sun grew brighter and his sight adjusted to the conditions he felt his stomach shrink – for now he could see the bulky shapes of the Catuvellauni charioteers still as stones. He could see *hundreds* of their charioteers and behind them *massed* foot-fighters. Had the Catuvellauni joined forces with the Trinovantes? They must have, for there were more chariots than he'd ever seen at one time before. More foot-fighters too and a *forest* of Catuvellauni spears.

Suddenly Topher realised that the Atrebates were horribly, horribly outnumbered. Doomed.

For when Catuvellauni spears met Atrebatan flesh ...
When Catuvellauni fire-arrows landed on Atrebatan thatches ...

He pictured the massacre even before he heard the battle howl of the Catuvellauni leader, before the line of enemy chariots surged forward. Seeing them, he closed his eyes and begged the gods to help.

'Gods of the forest, gods of the streams and rivers, help us!

Gods of the glades, gods of the fields and pastures, help us!

God of battles, help us!'

Then he hit the ground – as a spear whizzed over his head.

Thwunk! It sank in the post behind him.

Someone with brown arms was holding him down.

Someone with brown arms had pulled him down. He struggled to see a Roman boy, one he particularly hated. With brown curly hair he looked like a young bullock.

'Stay down, idiot!' he hissed in his foreign accent. 'Some of those natives can't aim straight. Or maybe they can.'

Above Topher's head the spear in the post was still vibrating.

'Let me go,' he managed to mutter.

'Only if you promise to lie low.'

'Of course I'll stay low, I'm not suicidal.'

'I'm glad to hear it.' The Roman boy loosened his

grip. 'Most of your tribe obviously is.'

He nodded in the direction of the battle. 'But watch the next bit. I think you will like it.'

Side by side on their stomachs now, the two boys watched the two armies bearing down on one another. The ground beneath them shook. Any moment now the two lines of chariots would clash. Already spears were flying into and over the charioteers of both sides. But two Atrebatan charioteers fell. Topher feared for his father and brother. A horse screamed in agony. Several of their foot-fighters fell. Yet the Catuvellauni were all upright and approaching fast.

'Look.' The Roman boy was pointing eastwards. 'Don't worry.'

Topher couldn't see anything to make him stop worrying.

'It's a *testudo*,' the boy said. 'There's another on the west side.'

Topher glanced again, but all he could see were the advancing Catuvellauni. Faster and faster, closer and closer they came, a relentless wave of destruction.

They looked unstoppable. First they would massacre the Atrebatan fighting men. Then they would flood through the northern gate or up and over the ramparts, their targets women, old men and children. Topher fought the fear racing through him. Then felt his rescuer – he supposed he must call him that – shaking his arm excitedly.

'Now! Look! See how your enemies are turning.'

The Catuvellaunian left flank did seem to be faltering,

did seem distracted by something. So did the right flank. In fact both flanks were swerving outwards to fight off a rain of iron bolts coming from the sides. The enemy were falling like skittles beneath the iron rain.

The Roman boy nudged Topher. 'Catapults, and in a moment the testudo! Now do you see?'

Looking to the left Topher saw red-crested helmets rising from the undergrowth. More helmets appeared from the right-hand side. He saw spears and shields in tight formations. He saw glittering shields. He saw the Roman army, the famous legionaries thrusting and slicing into the Catuvellauni who were falling to the ground like corn at harvest time. He saw the Roman standard bearer at their helm, holding high the bronze eagle, symbol of Roman power. He heard their trumpet call. Taranta-ta!

'See, we are not enemies. We are allies.' The smiling Roman boy thrust out his hand. 'Marcus, son of Cassius the mosaic-maker. What is your name?'

They didn't become friends straightaway. Topher had hated Marcus on sight – when he'd seen him working in the bathhouse, which occupied the ground where his family's roundhouse used to be. The Romans had destroyed their roundhouse. They had offered to replace it with a Roman-style house on the main street, but Bryn the Elder had declined. Proudly, he said he preferred to live in an Atrebatan house with others of his tribe, and had set up a compound of roundhouses near the north gate. The Roman rulers tried hard to get in with him, but

Bryn kept his distance. 'We shall be civil to them – as they say – and bide our time,' he told the family.

Topher found it hard to be civil. His brother found it hard to bide his time. He wanted to attack Roman property at least, but Bryn the Elder forbade that, even when a statue of the emperor appeared in the Forum, with the bronze eagle perched on his hand. Even when the Druid, high priest of the Atrebates, came out from his secret place in the woods to urge rebellion. He called on Bryn the Elder in the middle of the night. Topher remembered it well, waking up to the lilting voice of the strange bearded figure ordering his father to gather a fighting force and repel the invaders. He remembered feeling afraid as his father refused to take up arms against the Romans. 'There is no point,' he'd said. 'The Romans would simply kill us all.' The Druid said death was honourable and led to The Better Place, but his father would not be persuaded. There was no point in fighting the Romans *yet*, he said. They must wait till the tribe was stronger and had a chance of driving them out.

The battle with the Catuvellauni changed things. Bryn the Elder seemed to give up his dream of pushing out the Romans. We need them, he said, and became less critical of the Roman way of life, though he still lived in the roundhouse. The battle changed Topher too. He couldn't help feeling grateful to Marcus and the Romans for saving his life. Sometimes he stopped to watch them building the floors of the bathhouse. Their mosaics fascinated him. He loved the patterns and pictures they made, and one day he was able to help. Marcus was having trouble drawing the curving tail of a dolphin – he usually did straighter designs – so Topher drew it for him, even though he had never seen a dolphin! Marcus told him about these creatures which he'd seen on the voyage to Britain. And after that Marcus sometimes let him cut a few stones called *tesserae* and even place them in the mortar. He said Topher had a talent for it and Cassius, his father, agreed. He said Topher had a good eye for colour too. Soon after that he became an apprentice. Cassius taught him how to cut the stones correctly. Each one had to be flat at one end, sharp at the other.

'They must fit into mortar like teeth into gum,' he said, tapping Topher's teeth to make his meaning clear.

Bryn the Younger would have bitten his finger off. Bryn hated Topher working for the Romans. He thought Bryn the Elder was wrong to give permission. He was angered and disgusted by his father's changed attitude, though he hid his feelings in front of him. So Topher didn't suffer too much, not when his father was at home, but when Bryn the Elder went on a journey and didn't return, things got bad.

Chapter 12

'Has your father come back yet?' Marcus asked Topher one day, when Bryn the Elder had been gone nearly a week. They were in the portico of the bathhouse, where Topher was on his knees, chipping away at black tesserae.

'No,' he replied, wishing he could say more.

He was trying to learn the language of the Romans, but couldn't speak it well enough to explain how he was feeling, that he was worried about his father, afraid of his brother, and disturbed by what was happening outside. He didn't know why his father had gone, but thought it had something to do with the new road the Romans were building. It went past the bathhouse. All morning he'd listened to the sound of shovels and of Roman overseers ordering the Atrebatan road gang to work faster, faster. Whenever he looked up he'd seen the bowed backs of men who had been free a year ago.

Marcus left the portico suddenly, as his father, an older, plumper version of himself, came through from the changing room. Cassius picked up one of the stones and held it a moment between thumb and finger.

Topher waited.

'Good, good.' He put the stone down. 'But now I need white ones and . . . ' Now he frowned at Topher. 'You'd better step into the plunge bath before you cut any. Shower first – in the *frigidarium*!' He laughed as Topher got to his feet in a cloud of black dust. 'You Brits like the cold, don't you? Quick about it now! And get a haircut!' he yelled after him.

The shower was between two plunge baths and as he took off his dusty tunic, Topher decided to skip the cold bath. He wasn't as fond of bathing as the Romans. These leaf-fall days were nippy. There was no one else around, thank the gods. The ladies he'd heard earlier, splashing and shrieking, had gone, and so had the bathhouse slaves. He kept a lookout for Marcus though. Sneaking up and pushing Topher in the bath would be his idea of a joke.

But Marcus didn't appear till Topher was out of the shower, trying to pull his tunic over his dripping hair, wishing he could have it short like the Romans, and imagining his brother Bryn's reaction if he did.

'Topher, dirty beast!' Marcus was in the doorway, pointing to Topher's filthy tunic.

'You can't wear that to cut white tesserae! My father would go mad.'

'I haven't got another one.'

'Wait here,' said Marcus. 'And *dry* yourself while you're waiting.'

He threw Topher a cotton drying cloth and ran off. Seconds later he returned with permission from Cassius, to take Topher home and fetch a clean tunic.

'We can buy something to eat on the way from the *thermopolium*. The hot food shop,' he explained as they set off for the craft quarter.

'Will we see your catta?'

The catta was a wonderful animal, which sometimes

76

came to the baths with Marcus. For some reason Topher longed to see this animal again.

'Probably. Though she sometimes goes away without telling us. Come on, let's run.'

Topher didn't need persuading. He could already smell roast meat and baking bread. Running along the raised pavement they passed a temple, with a statue of Mithras slaying a bull, and soon reached the shops. In the thermopolium meat turned on a spit. In the next shop bread was piled high. Marcus ordered bread from one and sheep-meat on sticks from the other.

'*Thermopolium*. Hot food shop. *Pistrina*. Baker's.' Topher practised reading the shop signs as Marcus flipped a shiny coin.

'Minted especially for Vespasian,' he said, showing Topher the emperor's head on one side. 'To commemorate his ten years as emperor.'

Vespasian's statue was in the Forum, holding the bronze eagle which angered Bryn the Younger so much.

'See.' Marcus flipped the coin over, and showed Topher a horn of plenty on the other side. 'That means the empire is thriving. We are going through a period of great prosperity. We have never had it so good, friend Topher, so stick with us Romans and you'll thrive too! Come on!'

Handing the coin to the baker, he set off again at a run and the bread and meat were still warm when they got to the house cum workshop. Topher had never been in a Roman house before. It was strangely long and narrow, divided into many rooms. As he followed Marcus from the workshop at the front to the living quarters at the back, he was fascinated. But he was even more fascinated by the catta! There she was – on the floor of the living room sleeping, near the wall, a ball of golden fur, like no creature he had seen before. He couldn't take his eyes off her.

'Ca,' said Marcus. 'That's what we call her, because it's short for *catta* and it's like the Egyptian word for a double. Isn't she beautiful? She resembles Bastet, the Egyptian cat-goddess.'

He pointed out the key-like figure on her forehead, and said it was an Egyptian good luck sign, the sign of life itself in fact. Hearing her name or smelling the meat, Ca stirred and stretched. Then she stood up sticking her long tail in the air.

'Look.' Marcus stroked her head and she rubbed her cheeks against his brown hand, but she gazed at Topher with round shining eyes.

'She sleeps there because it's the warmest spot – where the hypocaust comes in. You know about our heating system, don't you? We have it in the bathhouse too. Ca loves it.'

The floor beneath Topher's bare feet was comfortingly warm, but he suddenly stepped back when the cat growled.

Marcus laughed. 'She's *purring*, not growling,' he said. 'It's a sign of contentment. She must like you. Stroke her like I did.'

Tentatively, Topher stroked the cat's head and the sound grew louder. He felt the sound beneath his fingers.

'By Jove. She likes you,' Marcus said, leaving the room.

She certainly seemed to. She was rubbing against his bare legs now, sending shivers of delight through him. He'd never felt fur so soft before. Marcus called out. 'Come and eat! I'm in the *atrium*!'

Ca led the way to the food, which was on a low table in the next room. Above them the sun shone through a square hole in the ceiling.

'The house-slave must have skived off,' said Marcus as Topher watched Ca lapping water from the pool beneath the hole.

'She's so beautiful,' Topher said.

'*Pulchrissima*,' said Marcus, 'very beautiful.'

She turned to look at Topher with round amber eyes. He held out a piece of meat and she came towards him.

'Where did you get her?' She was eating the meat now, from his fingers, daintily with small white teeth.

'In Pompeii, where we live. Lived. We have another one in our house there. At home we have many cats to guard our grain from rats. Ca followed us to the harbour and came aboard ship with us. By the time we noticed, Pater said it was too late to take her home.'

Pater, that meant father.

Mater meant mother. Marcus's mother and sisters were still in Pompeii. At least he hoped they were. There had been rumours of a disaster there.

'There were several cats on the ship. Sailors keep cats to keep rats away from the grain too. You must have seen a cat before, Topher?'

'Never, till Ca. What are rats?'

'Like large mice,' Marcus explained. 'But faster. Greedier. Pests, but quite tasty stuffed.' Then he went off to get Topher one of his spare tunics, saying the filthy one could go to the fuller's for a good cleaning.

Topher was watching a brilliant blue dragonfly hovering over the pool, when Ca started to lick his fingers with a surprisingly rough tongue. Looking down he saw her eyes change colour as cloud moved over the sun in the sky above. They changed shape too he noticed – one moment round, the next a sliver, then round again – like the moon, he thought. No wonder the Egyptians worshipped cats. Perhaps they worshipped the Moon Goddess too, like his tribe.

Marcus returned with a neatly pressed tunic, not too different from the one he'd taken off. It was brown. Hoping Bryn wouldn't notice the difference Topher put it on.

He asked, 'Do Romans worship cats?'

Marcus laughed. 'In a way. We Romans worship our gods and other people's – to be on the safe side.' He handed him a pair of sandals. 'Here, put these on too. I've grown out of them. Then we must be off.'

Ca followed them to the front door but didn't come with them to the bathhouse. She sat on the step and started to wash as they set off at a run. But when Topher glanced back for a last look, he saw that she was gazing at him.

He felt her eyes on him as he ran up the street.

'All you need now is a haircut,' Marcus said, as they

passed the barber's, 'and you could pass for a Roman, but hurry or my father will flog us both for being late.'

But Topher was more worried by his own brother than Marcus's father. He had reason too, though he took off the sandals before he reached the compound that night. Hiding them under a stone near the gate, he hoped Bryn wouldn't notice his tunic. But Bryn did as soon as he entered the roundhouse. Topher's heart sank when he saw his father still wasn't there. Bryn the Younger was sitting in his place by the central fire, where their mother, Gladwys, was stirring stew, with the sleeves of her russet robe rolled up above her elbows. When she flicked back her braided hair to stop it hanging in the pot, she noticed Topher, but Bryn pretended he hadn't seen him. He sniffed the air and said, 'I do believe a stinking Roman has crossed our threshold.'

Then he turned towards the door saying, 'Oh, it's you, little brother. How pretty you look! But is not Atrebatan cloth good enough for you now?'

Topher saw that Bryn had spiked his hair with lime in the old way and marked his forehead with blue dye.

'Mine got dirty. It's just being washed, that's all. I'll get it back tomorrow.'

'Washed! There's posh! And you look as if you've been washing yourself too. Had a nice Roman bath, have you!'

But there were more serious matters afoot, he said. Had Topher not heard how his Roman friends were going to violate their sacred space? Did he not know they were planning to build one of their godless roads across their sacred grove? They had started. It went past their stupid bathhouse. It was time to take sides, he said.

'Whose side are you on, little brother? Are you going to stay with your new Roman friends and betray your own kith and kin?'

Topher asked Bryn to explain, but at that point their younger sisters, Eluned and Enid, came in. Looking like miniatures of their mother, with their fair braided hair and russet robes they were carrying baskets of black-berries. As Gladwys glared and shook her head at him, Bryn said they would talk later. He tugged Eluned's plait. She told him she'd picked her blackberries for him.

Enid said, 'I have picked these for you, Topher.' Her mouth was purple and there were three blackberries in her basket, but he thanked her and she laughed. Their mother laughed too, briefly, then her strong face looked serious again as she handed Bryn a bowl of stew. Something was obviously the matter. What did Bryn mean? It was time to take sides.

Chapter 13

Topher had to wait to find out. After the evening meal of bread and stew they sat round the fire, while Bryn told them stories of their heroes – British heroes like Caradoc who had fought the Romans for eight long years, and Boudicca, the wonderful Boudicca. Queen of the Iceni tribe, she had massacred the Romans with her daughters' help. With her *daughters*, he'd repeated, holding the braids of Enid and Eluned as if they were the reins of a war horse. Enid giggled but Eluned looked fierce, as if she too would like to fight the Romans. So did their mother. The noble queen had died rather than pay tribute to the Romans, Bryn said, and he described Boudicca in her shining chariot, her golden hair streaming behind her as she led the Iceni into battle:

'Wielding sword and shield she led them,
Wondrous woman led woad-splashed warriors!'

As he spoke you could see the spike-haired warriors in their blue battle paint, hear their war horns and the thrum of the battle drums. The words were thrilling but Topher wished his father were here. Bryn the Elder said that thousands of Britons had been massacred during that rebellion, and the Romans had rebuilt the towns that Boudicca had destroyed. Nothing had been gained. And the Iceni were a war-loving tribe, enemies of the Atrebates before the Romans came. The Romans had in fact made things safer.

But Bryn the Younger could see no good in the Romans. 'Who needs *Roman* houses?' he was saying now, waving his bangled arm. Its shadow on the wattle wall made it look like the arm of a giant.

'Who needs *hypocaust*?' he said with a sneer. 'Who needs hot pipes? What could be better than this?'

Their mother smiled and handed him a beaker of ale, decorated with the swirling patterns of their tribe, and as the fire flickered, toasting their feet, Topher couldn't think of anything better. The wattle walls kept out the winds of leaf-fall. The fire flames didn't simply warm as they flickered and danced, they cheered the spirit too. But as the wood smoke spiralled up to the hole in the roof and onwards to the stars, Topher remembered winter nights when rain poured through that hole. When icy winds howled round the hut, lifting the thatch and shaking the skins over the doorhole. He remembered nights when they huddled together in the sleeping place shivering with cold, however many furs they piled on top of themselves. Roman heating was more reliable.

'Here, brother.' Bryn handed Topher his beaker of ale and watched him take a mouthful. 'Were you thinking about what I said earlier? We men must talk about these things.'

In the sleeping quarter on the other side of the roundhouse, their mother was smoothing the calfskins beneath the girls and covering them with sheep-pelts.

84

'May the gods protect you, daughters,' they heard her say.

'May they protect us all,' said Bryn, taking back his ale. 'But they will do so, only if we protect their sacred places.'

And then, as their mother joined them, he spoke again in hushed tones of the danger he'd mentioned earlier. Taking a stick, he drew a map of the town in the earth at their feet. He drew the seven sides and the network of straight roads that now stretched across it. He showed the old ramparts and the new ones built outside the old, because the town had grown bigger since the Romans came.

'This road,' he said, pointing to the one Topher had walked along that day, from the bathhouse to Marcus's. 'This *street* the Romans are building outside their bathhouse, the one that crosses the town westwards. It joins the Sorviodunum road, as they call it. Well, they plan to extend it eastwards now. They will put a new east gate there, and as I have said, the road will go straight through the sacred grove.'

Their mother made the sign of the moon, and so did Topher. He understood now. It was frightening news. The sacred grove was a circle of oaks where the Druid carried out the ancient rites. Where the rites *had* to take place to placate the gods.

'We haven't much time,' said Bryn. 'Samain is less than a moon away.'

Though he was close to the fire, Topher shivered. Samain was the night when evil spirits of the Other

85

World were let loose on the human world – and stayed if the Moon Goddess was angry. And she would be angry if the sacred grove was destroyed and she was not worshipped in the proper way. As Bryn poured dregs of ale onto a smouldering log it spluttered and blackened, showing what the gods could do – put out the fire, take away the sun and never return it. Already the sun stayed for a shorter time each day. Already the nights were getting longer and the ground colder. Leaves were falling from the trees and plants were dying. If the Druid didn't make the proper sacrifices in the proper place, the branches of the trees would stay bare, the earth would stay brown. The sun would go and never return.

'How can the Druid make the sacrifices to the Moon Goddess if the sacred grove is destroyed?' Bryn said, looking from his mother to Topher and back again.

Gladwys shook her head.

'So, we must stop the Romans.'

Their mother nodded in agreement and so did Topher. Of course. It was dangerous to anger the gods. The Romans must be stopped – he could see that. And they would stop, if they knew. Marcus said they worshipped their gods and other people's.

'Ouch!'

Bryn had poked him in the ribs. 'No word of this to your Roman friends, by the way. We want to surprise them.'

'B-but we must ask them!' Topher managed to say. 'We must ask the magistrate in charge of public works.'

Bryn spat into the fire. 'Ask! Do you think our father

didn't try to ask? Where do you think he is? No one in Calleva would listen so he has gone to *ask* Agricola, the Roman governor himself, who is visiting that stooge Cogidubnus. For a sennight we have waited for him to return.'

Cogidubnus was chief of the Durotriges, the tribe south of the Atrebates who had thrown in their lot with the Romans.

As Gladwys filled Bryn's beaker with ale, Topher tried to say that their father might be on his way back and that the Romans honoured all sorts of gods. Marcus was always saying, 'By Mithras this!' or 'By Isis that!' Mithras was from Persia. Isis was from Egypt. In the bathhouse there was a shrine to Fortuna, Lady Luck. The Romans had lots of sacred places. If they knew about the sacred grove, they would change their route. It was a matter of speaking to the right person. He was sure of it. But neither Bryn nor Gladwys would listen. Bryn said time was short and plans had been made. They must surprise the Romans and give them a taste of their own medicine. When Topher tried to argue Bryn sent him to the sleeping place to warm it.

Usually the click and swish of his mother's shuttle – as she wove plaid at the loom lulled Topher to sleep, but not tonight. The sight of Bryn getting drunk didn't help. What was he planning to do? When he came to the sleeping place, Topher again suggested asking the Romans to re-route the road, but Bryn scoffed.

'*Ash-k* them to put a bend in one of their so straight streets? *Ash-k* them to honour our gods?'

And before Topher could answer, he had pulled the sheepskin over his head. As Topher watched his mother leave her loom and go to bank up the fire, he wished that their father would come home. If Bryn the Younger was planning to do something stupid, only Bryn the Elder could stop him. Soon only the dullest of glows shone from the fire. They never let it go out if they could help it. It was hard to light it again and without fire they would die of cold. Without the sun and moon they would all perish.

As Gladwys settled in her sleeping place the hay beneath her rustled. Then the roundhouse fell silent and he lay in the darkness thinking. What could he do to prevent a disaster? If Bryn stirred up a rebellion the Romans would put it down ruthlessly. They could be cruel, would be cruel – and the gods would still be angry because the Romans would go ahead and build their road through the sacred grove.

Early next morning, before anyone else was awake, Topher crept out of the compound. Bryn would call it treachery, but he had to warn the Romans. He had to ask them to re-route their road to save the tribe from disaster.

Chapter 14

Picking up his sandals from beneath the stone where he'd left them, he headed for the craft quarter – to ask Cassius for help. Cassius knew the magistrate in charge of public works who could stop the road if he wanted to. He was the man to ask.

It wasn't long before he reached the silent Forum where most of the shops still had their shutters up. Veils of early morning mist still shrouded the statue of the emperor in the middle of the square, but you could just see the eagle on his hand. As Topher ran across the cobbles his bare feet slip-slapped loudly, but soon he was where he wanted to be, on the corner opposite Marcus's house. What now? The shutters were up, the door closed. Should he cross the street and knock on the door or wait for someone to come out? Were Cassius and Marcus still inside? Sometimes they started work very early. As he wondered what to do, the wondrous Ca came out of the alley at the side of their house.

Seeing him, she crossed the street tail held high.

'*Salve*, Ca!' he said softly, stroking her head as she rubbed her silky fur against his legs and patted the leather thong dangling from the sandal in his hand. 'Where are they, Ca? Where's Marcus?'

And – it was amazing – she stopped playing and looked up at him with round amber eyes. Then as the mist lifted and the sun appeared in the eastern sky, she took off, in long leaps towards the sun and the bathhouse. Delighted he ran after her, but his delight turned to dismay. Before he reached the baths he saw wooden stakes marking the route of the new road, which went straight to the heart of the sacred grove. Clearly the gods were already angry. The sky was on fire. The black oaks crowning the hill looked as if they were burning.

'Mwow!'

Ca was looking up at him.

He hadn't realised he had stopped.

'Mwow!'

Her voice was urgent and urging. *Come on, Topher. Hurry.*

As they reached the bathhouse, he saw the road-gang already digging ditches along the line of the stakes. And with the gang and the overseers were a couple of Roman legionaries, strutting like cockerels in their red-crested helmets. As one of the gang straightened his back a legionary ordered him to work. Another legionary shouted at Topher, 'On your way, you long-haired girl!'

Hurrying into the bathhouse, Topher saw Cassius in the portico measuring something. Today there was no cheerful *Salve*! He didn't look up as he ordered Topher to get working.

Topher started to say, 'But there is a matter of importance ... '

But Cassius didn't listen. He strode off to another part of the baths. There was no sign of Marcus or Ca now. Perhaps she had gone to find him. As Topher began to chip away at a pile of shale – he thought it best to obey his master – he kept eyes and ears open. He must speak to Cassius or even Marcus soon. Trouble was brewing outside. The legionaries were shouting insults at the Atrebates. 'Move your feet, stinking Celts! Get a move on, idle Brits!'

If Bryn wanted to start a rebellion, he'd find willing followers. The mood inside was different too. Even the slaves didn't speak to him. The women who usually came to the baths in the morning didn't arrive. Cassius didn't come back. Nor did Ca.

When Marcus did appear at lunchtime, something was obviously wrong. He was with Cassius and they were both rushing out of the door into the street. As Marcus ran after his father he said something to Topher about Vulcan, one of their gods, being angry. Topher managed to say, 'Yes, and our gods will be angry too if . . . ' But that was all. Marcus had gone, urged on by his father.

Topher grew desperate. He had to do something – quickly. Why all this rushing about? Had Bryn done something already? He got more news from Decius, one of the slaves, whom he found in the hot room when he went looking for Ca. Ca was okay. Decius was feeding her with small pieces of cheese, which she loved. But Decius wasn't okay. None of the slaves were. They sat, head in hands some of them, on the edge of the bath. Decius said there had been a dreadful disaster back home. Pompeii, a town where some of them came from, had been destroyed by a volcano. A mountain had exploded and fire had destroyed the whole town. Vulcan must be very angry with them. It was terrible.

Things started to make a bit of sense. Pompeii was where Marcus and his father used to live, where his mother and sisters still lived – or had lived. No wonder they weren't behaving normally. Decius said they were at the temple offering sacrifices to the gods.

It was mid afternoon when they returned and Topher was back in the portico working. Ca was with him, sleeping on a warm piece of floor, but when Marcus stopped to say they'd been to the temple of Jove, because there was no shrine to Vulcan in Calleva, she woke up. Marcus said he and Cassius had also been to Venus's shrine, to ask her to protect his *mater* and sisters. His voice faltered slightly and Topher nodded to show he understood, but Cassius snapped, 'Act like a Roman, not a sentimental Brit.'

He ordered them both to get on with their work. Marcus, with Ca at his heels, headed for the back of the building. All Topher could do that day was pray to his own gods, to protect the sacred grove and bring his father home soon. He didn't see Cassius or Marcus or Ca any more that day.

When he reached the compound at nightfall, Bryn the Younger was just inside the gate talking quietly to Deri, another young man of the tribe. Like Bryn, Deri had spiked his long hair with lime and painted his forehead blue. When they saw Topher they stopped talking. Clearly something was afoot. Later, Bryn said he and Deri had been to see the Druid, who had approved their plan. The Druid, who lived in the woods, hated the Romans.

'What plan?' Topher said.

But Bryn tapped his nose. 'If you don't know, you can't tell your Roman friends, can you, little brother?'

Topher felt more worried than ever, but at least there was still time to do something. He should have made Cassius listen today. Cassius – and lots of the Romans – obviously had problems of their own, but keeping quiet about the road would not make things better. In fact, it could make things worse. So after the evening meal, Topher crept out of the compound once again and headed for his master's house.

Chapter 15

Leaving the roundhouse at night wasn't unusual. Nature's calls had to be answered and Atrebatans didn't have disgusting inside latrines. Leaving the compound was trickier. If Bryn saw him leaving, he'd want to know why. And Topher had to be quick. He must get back before Bryn got suspicious. It was dark in the compound. Cloud covered the moon but it was a bit lighter on the street. As he ran past a line of Roman houses, he glimpsed a red glow and sometimes a shower of sparks – from the furnaces, which fed the hypocaust. He saw slaves playing knucklebones as they tended the furnaces. Woe to them if they let the fires go out.

Every now and then a dog barked. Once, as he ran past the high wall of the Basilica, an owl floated past like a small white ghost. He kept running though, through the cold night air, which smelt of grilled fish. He pictured the Romans inside their houses, heard them from time to time eating and drinking. What would Cassius and Marcus be doing? What should he do when he got there? Knock on the front shutter or go round the back? He was still wondering when he arrived at the corner opposite their house. The workshop was in darkness, the shutters up, but there was a glow from the tile shop next door. He could see the sturdy silhouette of Mentinus the tiler, holding up a tile. Then suddenly Mentinus was in the street.

'Confounded cat!'

Ca streaked past and something landed at Topher's feet.

Then Marcus appeared from the alley between the two shops and Mentinus was grabbing him, pulling him into the shop and pointing angrily.

'What have you done, Ca?' said Topher, feeling fur against his legs. 'Don't worry, I'll look after you.' He picked her up and stayed in the shadows till Mentinus went inside. Then he heard Marcus calling softly for Ca.

'She's here.' With Ca in his arms he stepped into the street.

'Is she all right?'

'I think so. I don't think he hit her.'

'She stepped on one of his damp tiles,' said Marcus. 'She was probably chasing a mouse. His house is full of them.' He scratched behind her ear and she started to purr.

'He ought to be grateful.'

Topher could feel the vibrations of her body.

'You're a good cat, aren't you, Ca?' said Marcus.

'What's all this?' Now Cassius appeared yawning. Topher remembered his mission.

'Excuse me, master, but I have to talk to you.'

They went inside where the remains of the evening meal were still on the low table. Ca started to lick one of the dishes.

'Fish sauce,' said Marcus laughing, but his father told him to be silent. Vicus, the slave, started to clear away the dirty dishes and Topher began.

*

Titus Adonicus was the man to see, Cassius said, when Topher finished telling him about the road, which he managed to do without mentioning Bryn. He wanted to stop trouble not cause it. Titus Adonicus was the magistrate in charge of public works. Unfortunately he lived in a villa outside the town. That was part of the problem, Cassius said. Magistrates had taken to living in villas in the country, where they quickly lost touch with what was going on in town.

'I'll go and see him tomorrow,' Cassius said. 'This is urgent. You were right to come.'

'Tomorrow! You must go now!'

Marcus gave him a warning glare. Cassius stood up. It was time for Topher to leave, he said. Marcus came outside with him.

'He will go – at first light. He can't go now, Topher. It would be too dangerous. Finding a country villa in the dark is almost impossible.'

He said roads, where they existed, weren't clearly marked and you could be attacked by wolves or bears or bandits.

Topher raced back to the compound, only slightly less worried. Before he reached the fence he could hear the rise and fall of Bryn's story-telling voice. It was Boudicca again. As he walked into the roundhouse, pulling down his tunic, as if he had been relieving himself, Bryn, facing the door, saw him enter. So did Gladwys their mother, who sat beside him, rippling the strings of her small harp. With them round the fire were his sisters and others of the tribe, Bryn's friends among them. When Bryn came to the end of his story the party broke up. Topher saw his brother exchange a glance with Deri before he stepped into the night.

'Get you to bed, boy.' Gladwys saw him watching and nodded towards Enid and Eluned who were already in the sleeping place. Soon afterwards, after banking up the fire, she went and lay near them. Topher saw her pull a plaid over herself. The place where she usually slept with his father lay empty.

Bryn didn't come to bed at first. He sat by the fire stirring the ashes with a stick. What plans had he and his friends made? There had been talk earlier in the evening of refusing to work for the Romans, but Bryn had ruled that out. At last he heaved himself onto the hassock beside Topher, who pretended to be asleep.

'Where did you go tonight then, little brother?'

When Topher didn't reply Bryn pulled their sheepskin over himself. Still Topher pretended to be asleep, and possibly because Bryn didn't start snoring as he usually did, he went to sleep. But he woke at first light hearing someone coming in the door. His father? His heart leaped at first – then sank again.

It was Bryn. He felt the place beside him. It was cold. So Bryn must have been gone for some time. He was pulling off his boots. Where had he been? What had he been doing? Relieving himself? He didn't usually put on his boots to do that. Again Topher pretended to be asleep – somehow he thought that was best – and shortly afterwards he felt Bryn lying down beside him, carefully now as if he didn't want to disturb him. Soon after that he began to snore. Then the trumpet from the garrison west of the town sounded cockcrow. Then a real cockerel crowed and the dawn chorus began. Where had Bryn been? What had he been up to? Topher felt uneasy. The racket of birds, Bryn's snoring and worry made getting back to sleep impossible.

Easing himself out of the sleeping place, he pulled on his outer garments. If Cassius had set off at first light he would be on his way by now. Marcus would have got up early too, to start work at the bathhouse. It would be good to see his friend. As he lifted the skin over the door Topher noticed Bryn's muddy boots. Some of the mud was red-brown. Where had that come from? The earth in the compound was yellow-brown.

Outside all was quiet except for a few hens scratching and a dog peeing against a drying rack. Most of the livestock were still asleep. The ox opened a wrinkled eye. The dog came and sniffed him, but it made no objection when he went out through the gate. Still hoping that Cassius would be in time to prevent whatever trouble Bryn had planned or, even worse, begun, Topher was soon running down Forum Street. What he saw in the Forum brought him to a sudden halt.

Chapter 16

The bronze eagle had gone!

The eagle, symbol of Roman power, had been removed from the hand of the emperor! Afterwards Topher thought he should have raced straight home and begged his brother to return it instantly, before anyone discovered it had gone. Why didn't he? Because he wasn't sure Bryn had stolen it? Because he feared Bryn's response? Because he hoped that the eagle had been removed for cleaning perhaps? He raced instead to the bathhouse and burst in on Marcus in the *caldarium*.

'The s-statue – have you seen it?'

Marcus, carefully putting the eye in his dolphin mosaic, didn't answer.

'The eagle in the emperor's hand – it's gone!' Topher almost screamed.

Then Marcus looked up, brown eyes alarmed. 'What do you mean?'

'Could it have been removed – for cleaning or something?'

Marcus shattered his last hope. 'No. It would be bad luck to remove it.'

Bad luck. Bad fortune. There was a shrine to the goddess Fortuna in the *tepidarium* next door where the Romans sometimes played dice. No good could come without good luck. That's what Romans believed. If Lady Luck was against you, you were doomed.

Marcus shook his head. 'Who would do such a thing? Who would violate the statue of a god?'

The Romans worshipped the emperor too, Topher remembered. He kept silent. Now slaves were arriving, from their quarters behind the bathhouse. He could hear them. They wouldn't have seen the statue yet, but the town was waking up. Soon someone would see it, and then? Topher felt sick.

'My father's mission is a waste of time then,' said Marcus bleakly – and as he spoke they heard the garrison trumpet sounding the alert. Soon after that they heard the east gate crashing shut. On all sides of the town gates would be closing, making them all prisoners.

Marcus rushed to the portico, with Topher close behind. The fat bathhouse keeper was already there. So was a cluster of slaves – all anxiously looking up and down the street. Suddenly a man ran out of the strong-house opposite. The strong-house was where Romans kept their valuable things and important papers. Lucius, the keeper, obviously expected a riot or robbers. Calling for slaves to guard the door, he headed down the street towards the Forum, clutching his toga above his knees. Slaves rushed out with an iron grille. As they fixed it over the door the trumpet sounded the alert again. It was louder this time and nearer, coming from the Forum perhaps. It was followed by an announcement. Topher guessed what it was from the shocked faces round him. He felt his pulses racing.

Then Lucius was galloping back up the street.

'The imperial eagle has been stolen! The eagle's been stolen!'

The slaves opened the grille, let him in, and closed it with a clash.

Then a gang of Atrebatans appeared at a run with knees held high, though they carried picks and shovels over their shoulders. With them were legionaries, shouting orders and cracking whips. Topher stepped back as the gang passed the bathhouse, heading eastwards. When he looked out again he saw them nearly at the ramparts. He noticed that a stretch of road had already been built.

'HALT, SCUM!' roared a legionary. 'DIG, SCUM!'

Lifting their picks, the gang started to dig more of the ditches that would line the street to the sacred grove. And the legionaries set a furious pace, beating time with a drum. Then – it must have been a relief at first – a centurion on horseback appeared.

'HALT!'

As the gang downed tools, the crowd in the portico moved along the road a bit, straining to hear more. They heard the centurion demanding information about the eagle, saying the reward for co-operation would be great, the punishment for withholding information severe. As he moved down the line of Atrebatans, barking at each one, 'What do you know?' – he got closer to the bathhouse and Marcus tugged Topher's arm.

'Come on. You'd better keep your head down,' he said as he bundled him back into the bathhouse. 'Till my father returns.'

Wishing his own father would return – and that he'd

never gone away, Topher followed him to the *caldarium* at the back. It was safer, Marcus said, than being on view at the front. All Atrebatans were under suspicion. Arrests would be made. Decimation might be the result.

'If they think people are withholding information, the authorities will start to kill one in ten Atrebatans, till they find the culprit,' he explained. Then he told Topher to finish the dolphin's tail, adding that Brits were good at curved designs. He was trying to cheer him up. Topher realised that, but it didn't work. Topher couldn't forget his worries and nor could Marcus.

'I hope my father will return soon,' he said.

'I hope he will,' said Topher. 'And that my father will.'

Had Bryn taken the eagle? It looked likely. Would he confess to save other lives?

They heard some Roman ladies arriving and the keeper apologising because they could not use the *caldarium*. He said the *tepidarium* was hotter than usual and he hoped they would forgive the inconvenience. Soon they heard the women's voices amid the splashes, talking of the day's events – and yesterday's. Topher had forgotten about the disaster in Pompeii. They hadn't and nor had Marcus of course. Like the women he saw connections – the gods were angry and now they would be even angrier, he said. 'The eagle isn't just a symbol of Roman power,' he explained. 'It is an attribute of Jupiter himself. It held his thunderbolt in its talons. There will be death and destruction here in Calleva if the eagle isn't returned.'

Again Topher kept quiet. What could he do to prevent disaster? Betray his own brother?

It was mid morning when Cassius returned to the bathhouse. He said the two magistrates in charge of public works had returned to Calleva with him. Concerned by what he told them, they had come straightaway. Unfortunately, they were already too late. Now an emergency meeting of the full council was taking place in the Basilica. The military were in control of the town, awaiting further orders from the council. The town was swarming with soldiers and a messenger was on his way to Camulodunum, the capital, to tell Agricola, the Governor of Britannia. Cassius told Topher to borrow some clean Roman clothes from Marcus and smarten himself up.

'The council wants to question you immediately. I had to tell them where I got my information. You would do well to look like a friend of Rome. I wish there was time to take you to the barber's but there isn't. We'd better tie your hair back.'

As Topher walked through the town wearing Marcus's best white tunic, Cassius at his side, there were soldiers on every corner. There were more in the Forum where a soothsayer was wailing about death and destruction. Feeling hostile glances from everyone they met, Topher thought desperately about what to say and tried not to show his fear.

Chapter 17

A flight of steps led up to the Basilica. As Cassius explained to the legionaries guarding the doors why they had come, Topher glanced behind him. In the Forum below stood the huge statue of the emperor, his hand outstretched and empty. Now, too late, soldiers guarded it.

'Come on,' said Cassius as the doors opened and they stepped into a vast room, the biggest room Topher had ever seen. A forest of carved pillars held up the long ceiling. 'Show great respect to the council, up there, in the apsidal,' said Cassius, pointing to a half-circle at the far end of the room. Another flight of steps led up to it and the council looked down from it, ten Roman elders in white togas, looking as if they were carved out of stone. Then the one in the centre moved his hand and a voice said, 'Let the boy approach!'

Cassius nudged him. 'That's Marcus Aulus, the magistrate in charge of justice,' he said. He pushed a strand of hair behind Topher's ear and nodded encouragingly. 'Call him noble sir. Show respect but not fear. Go on.'

Wishing his master could come with him, Topher began the long walk to the foot of the steps. As soon as he reached them Marcus Aulus beckoned again and he climbed the steps – till he was standing directly in front of the magistrates. They sat at a stone table looking on severely.

'Topher son of Bryn?' Marcus Aulus had a shiny bald pate, but his eyes and nose were like a hawk's.

'Yes, noble sir.'

'Cassius, the mosaic-maker, tells us you are a friend of Rome.'

'Yes, noble sir.'

'And that you tried to warn us about the sacrilege that has taken place?'

'Yes, noble sir.'

'How did you learn of this?'

'I heard talk, noble sir.'

'From whom?'

'People, sir.'

'Topher.' Hawk Nose leaned over the table. 'Tables don't talk. We know *people* told you. We want to know *which ones*.'

What could he say?

Hawk Nose tapped his fingers on the table and breathed heavily.

'Who? Speak, boy!' This came from the magistrate on Hawk Nose's left.

Hawk Nose spoke again, quickly now. 'Topher son of Bryn, we understand that your father – by-passing our authority – has gone to consult Cogidubnus of the Durotriges tribe, who will give him good counsel. But . . . '

The magistrate on his right whispered something in his ear.

Hawk Nose continued, speaking even faster. 'Topher son of Bryn, the matter is urgent and you are a friend of Rome. We therefore think it right to tell you that we suspect your brother, Bryn, and have taken steps to arrest him. Unfortunately he has fled which seems to confirm his guilt. Do you know where he is?'

Topher shook his head.

'We have received a message in bad Latin, saying the eagle will be melted down unless we agree to stop building the road to your sacred grove. We have taken measures to prevent this, of course, but these measures will cause great hardship. Fires and furnaces are now forbidden. There will be no lighting, cooking, heating or smelting within a forty mile area till the eagle is found. You know what this means?'

Topher did know. It was terrible news. Winter was fast approaching. Without fire people would die of cold and hunger. But worse was to come. Hawk Nose was still speaking. 'Secondly, we have arrested your mother and sisters, as a precaution. We trust that your brother will return the eagle and accept punishment like a man, rather than see his own kin suffer.'

'Suffer?'

'Suffer.'

Topher couldn't believe what he was hearing.

'So we're sure you will help us, Topher. Tell us where your brother is.' Hawk Nose smiled but it wasn't a friendly smile. 'Tell us where the eagle is,' he went on.

Topher shook his head miserably.

'You refuse to help us?' The smile vanished.

'No! I want to help,' Topher replied quickly, struggling to put his thoughts into words. He'd always wanted to help. That's why he'd gone to Cassius. He said so. 'I thought if you knew how important the sacred grove was to us, you would change the direction of the road to avoid it. You wouldn't want to offend our gods.'

'You were right,' said Hawk Nose. 'It was logical thinking, worthy of a Roman – at the time. Unfortunately that time has passed. It is too late. Your brother's action has changed things. Rome cannot give in to threats from subject peoples.'

Topher couldn't help flinching at that.

'Find the eagle – that is our priority. I repeat, do you know where it is?'

Topher shook his head again.

'Do you know where your brother is? Speak up, boy!'

'No, noble sir.'

Hawk Nose stood up. 'Cassius the mosaic-maker!'

As Cassius walked the length of the hall, Topher wondered what was going to happen. 'Cassius, we are putting Topher son of Bryn in your charge – temporarily. Treat him as a friend of Rome. Discuss these matters with him. You, boy, use this time wisely. Think where your brother might be. Think where he may have hidden the eagle. Think of your mother and sisters. Great misery will result if the eagle is not found. When you can suggest where we look, inform us immediately. Cassius the mosaic-maker, you must bring Topher here at day-break tomorrow at the latest – *with helpful information*. Do you both understand?'

'Yes, noble sir,' said Cassius.

'Yes, noble sir,' said Topher.

'Then you are dismissed.'

'Cheer up,' said Cassius when, at last, they were outside

the Basilica, walking down the steps into the Forum. 'It could have been worse. They could have arrested you as well. They've given you time instead.'

'What for?'

'To change your mind, of course. Help them. I'm supposed to help change it, Topher, let you know how unpleasant they can be if you don't co-operate. You do know how they get information from people reluctant to give it?'

Topher nodded. Torture. His own people also used such methods.

'Think hard, Topher. Your brother needs to know that he has put the lives of his family in great danger. Your mother and sisters could die if he doesn't return the eagle.'

As they walked across the Forum, still watched closely by legionaries, Topher thought hard. What had Bryn done with it? Where might he have hidden it? Where had he been last night? Suddenly he remembered Bryn's muddy boots. Now he wished he'd examined the mud more closely. It might give a clue as to where Bryn had been, where he had hidden the eagle. There might be more clues. He told Cassius, who said they must go back to the compound.

There were legionaries at the compound gate. Cassius had to get permission for Topher to enter. When he did a legionary marched alongside him, for his own protection he said. Topher immediately saw why. From a scene of chaos came hisses and hostile glares. In their search for Bryn and the eagle soldiers had destroyed everything. They'd pulled down roof thatches, ripped holes in walls, turned over wagons and smashed storage pots. Collapsed buildings, animal skins, foodstuffs and upturned buckets covered the ground. Topher tried to meet the eyes of his neighbours, blood kin most of them. He wanted to show them how upset he was, but many turned their backs on him. Some just looked at their feet. Ffynn, the smith, stood by the blackened ashes of his furnace, trying to soothe a pony. Gryff, the potter, standing by his kiln, spat as Topher walked by. The curfew was already in place. A smell of soot hung in the air and ash floated in puddles. Hens roosted in trees. The hissing grew louder as he made his way towards the family roundhouse. He saw the family dog cowering under an upturned cart. It wasn't fair. This was all Bryn's fault, not his.

The family roundhouse was a heap of wood and wattle. Sleeping place, cooking place, storage place – he couldn't tell them apart. His mother's loom lay broken, her harp nearby. Hay from ripped sleeping hassocks covered broken pots and torn garments. Beneath one heap he found Enid's wooden doll. Putting it in the folds of his tunic, he left the compound angry, frustrated and desperately worried. He had to get a message to Bryn to tell him about the danger their mother and sisters were in. Surely, when he knew, he'd give the eagle back? He wouldn't let his mother and sisters die.

But how could he tell him when he had no idea where he was?

Chapter 18

'Hold your head up!' Cassius snapped, as they walked to the bathhouse. 'Walk proudly. You've done nothing to be ashamed of, I hope.'

Topher obeyed, but felt ashamed. Everyone blamed him because of Bryn. The streets were full of angry people. Some of them hissed at him. Romans, Romano-Atrebatans and Atrebatans all saw him as a trouble-maker. Many Atrebatans loved the Roman way of life, especially the entertainments in the amphitheatre. Nobody wanted war to break out. Angry smiths stood by their empty forges. Scowling bakers stood by their cold ovens. The hot food shops were closed. A cold leaf-fall day hinted at worse to come. Dark clouds threatened rain. If the eagle wasn't found before winter people would die of starvation and cold.

Cassius set a fast pace. They still had the floors to finish he said. Work must go on, but he urged Topher to think hard. The situation was serious he said – as if Topher didn't know! The Romans wanted peace. They were reasonable people, prepared to co-operate and compromise as long as people co-operated and compromised with them. He went on about the Pax Romana. But they would stop at nothing to get the result they wanted. Bryn's action could cause a war, he said as they passed another angry smith turning away an even angrier farmer who couldn't get his tools mended.

Topher tried desperately to think. Bryn wouldn't destroy the eagle, not at first. He'd been stupid enough to think that the Romans would bargain with him, give in to his threat. He might still believe that. So where had he hidden it? In the woods most likely! As a hunter he knew the woods well. He was probably hiding there himself.

'But where exactly in the woods?' said Cassius when Topher told him. 'The woods cover miles.'

Calleva was surrounded by woods and heathland. Soldiers would have started searching them already, Cassius said. If they were just searching for Bryn they'd have started burning them down by now. That's what they usually did to drive out fugitives. Fear of melting the eagle at the same time was stopping them. Topher said he thought Bryn would keep moving.

They worked at the bathhouse till the light failed, then set off for home – Marcus's home. Cassius walked ahead of the boys, cursing the darkness as he stepped in dung or bumped into things. The streets were full of farmers leading livestock back to their shelters. Marcus said Cassius was angry because Topher wasn't being more helpful. He should have come up with something by now. Cassius wasn't looking forward to returning to a cold house and a cold meal. He wasn't looking forward to taking Topher to the council next morning. If Topher didn't tell the magistrates something useful – then or before then – Cassius would be in trouble too.

Ca was on the doorstep when they reached the workshop. Her eyes gleamed out of the darkness. She followed them inside when Vicus, the house slave, opened the door. Vicus led the way to a room at the back where he had laid out a meal. He had lit a small oil lamp too. By its welcome light they could just see bread, cheese, fruit and Vicus pointed proudly to some grilled lamb from the thermopolium. He'd got it just before the shop closed he said. He'd kept it warm by wrapping it in hay. There was red wine from Spain to drink. Cassius insisted they put out the lamp. There were probably guards all around he said. Without the lamp they could just see the shapes of each other in the darkness. Vicus filled his master's goblet and Cassius drank deeply. Stretched out on the couch like a noble Roman, he kept his cloak wrapped round him. He had been up at first light, he reminded them, and he was very tired.

Marcus sat on something called a sella – it was like a stool with sides – but Topher stayed standing, unsure of what to do. Then Marcus told him to sit beside him. Vicus, who was talkative and not as humble as Topher expected a slave to be, served Cassius with food and drink. He served Marcus – and when Cassius told him to – he served Topher too. As they ate, the slave boasted about the battles he'd won in the food queues while getting food for them all. Cassius laughed till the slave started blaming the stupid Atrebatans for causing the trouble. Cassius told him to shut up and fetch more wine. When he was out of the room Cassius said, 'Topher, you must think of something to tell the council tomorrow. Protecting your brother is not an option. It's either his life or your mother and sisters' lives.'

Topher said, 'I'm not protecting him. I really don't know where he is.'

Then Vicus came in with an amphora of wine.

All through the meal Ca sat near Topher, looking up at him, her moon-like eyes shining out of the shadows. She didn't like the cold either. Her warm spot on the floor, where the hot pipes came in from the furnace, had already gone cold. Cassius told him to ignore the animal, but when Cassius fell asleep towards the end of the meal, she grew bolder. She reached up with a paw and patted his hand.

Marcus said, 'She wants food. It's your own fault. You shouldn't have fed her last time you were here. Don't give her any. She's getting fat. She looks as if she may be having kittens in fact. That male-cat from the thermopolium was round here a week or so ago. And have some more meat yourself. Who knows when we'll get any more?'

Cassius began to snore. Topher was taking a piece of lamb when Ca jumped onto his knee. Vicus sniggered, 'The Brit is scared. He thinks it's a wild cat.'

Marcus said, 'Of course he isn't. Look.'

Ca was on Topher's knee, tucking her paws beneath her. He put his hand near her mouth and she licked his greasy fingers with her rough tongue. Then she began to purr – and for a few moments he almost forgot his worries. Almost. It was such a comforting sound. If only he could get word to Bryn about his mother and sisters. Where was Bryn?

Marcus broke into his thoughts. 'You've got to think

of something to tell the council. There will be trouble if you don't – for all of us. Tell me again what you saw last night.'

Topher told him about Bryn coming into the roundhouse and taking off his muddy boots. The mud was reddish brown – he thought – clay possibly. It had been very sticky. Marcus agreed that it was a clue, the only one they had. He asked if there were any leaves or twigs stuck to the clay. Topher couldn't remember. The colour was important though. It could indicate the direction Bryn had taken. There were several clay-pits around Calleva all with slightly different coloured clay. Where had the stuff on Bryn's boots come from? As he thought, Topher stroked Ca's silky back and she flexed her forepaws, dropping dry mud from her sickle-shaped claws onto his white tunic. He could just make out the colour, reddish brown – from the tile she'd trodden on. Could it be the same as the wet clay he'd seen on Bryn's boots? The cat turned round and looked up at him with intelligent eyes. Was she telling him something? Now thoughts came quickly.

'Where's Mentinus's tile-yard?' he said. 'The main one, not the little workshop next door?'

'East of the town,' said Marcus 'There's a clay-pit by the east gate. Why?'

Topher hesitated, aware that guards were probably listening. Then he whispered, 'I think Bryn went that way last night.'

'What makes you think that?' Marcus lowered his voice too.

114

'The colour of the mud on his boots. I think it's the same as the clay in Ca's claws. He may have gone to the Druid's,' said Topher to whom it suddenly seemed obvious. That's where Bryn must be hiding! The Druid had a secret hut, in the woods east of the town. He'd been there once with Bryn, to get healing herbs when their mother was ill. They'd left the town by the east gate and passed a tilemaker's on the way. They had entered the wood, by a particular tree, a V-shaped ash tree. From there, Bryn had followed a well-hidden path to the Druid's. He'd said Topher must memorise the path, in case he ever needed to come alone. Topher's heart began to beat fast. Could he find it again – in the dark? And get back again by morning?

Marcus said, 'Don't go. Tell my father. Tell the council, so the army can go and get him.'

'No,' said Topher. 'I couldn't explain how to get there. And if I took soldiers there, Bryn or the Druid, or both, would be sure to hear us. If they saw me, with even one Roman, they'd vanish – with the eagle if they've got it. I'm more likely to find it if I go alone.'

The more he thought about it, the more convinced he became, though the woods would be terrifying in the dark. It was nearly Samain. At this time of year evil spirits were on the loose. But he had to go alone. He had to find Bryn and persuade him to return the eagle.

Marcus tried to persuade him not to. 'What if you're not back by morning? My father will be in trouble and it could make things worse for your mother and sisters.'

'I will be back by morning.'

'You really think you can get the eagle back?' Marcus said at last.

'I've got to try – for my mother and sisters' sake. My father would never forgive me if I didn't try. We Atrebatans have our honour too.'

'Then I'm coming with you,' said Marcus. 'You'll need my help to get out of the town secretly. I know it better than you. The place is swarming with soldiers.'

'No. It'll be harder for two to get out and I've already told you if Bryn sees a Roman he'll vanish.'

'I'll make sure he doesn't see me. I won't let them see I'm Roman. I'll cover my head with a cloak.'

Topher thought about it. It would be less terrifying with two of them and Marcus could hide while he went on to the sacred place.

Cassius was still sleeping, snoring loudly now, his mouth wide open. With luck, Marcus said, he might sleep for the rest of the night on the couch. He did sometimes when he was very tired. Marcus said again that they must be back before morning. He didn't want his father to suffer.

'What about Vicus?'

Marcus went to the kitchen to see. When he came back he said the slave was asleep too. He'd got up early to see his father off, and he'd probably helped himself to wine. Marcus got a stylus and wax tablet and wrote a message for his father. While he did that Topher checked front and back of the house. Both were guarded. Five minutes later, they climbed onto the roof through the hole in the atrium. They made their way over the rooftops as silently as they could, till they were well away from the craft quarter. Then they dropped down into the dark street.

Chapter 19

Wrapped in grey hooded cloaks, they hoped to merge with the shadows, as they headed east, moving as swiftly as they could while keeping a lookout. At first Marcus led the way, because he knew the town well. Sliding down dark alleys, he avoided streets where possible. There were armed soldiers on every corner, more patrolling the streets and open spaces. Cloud cover helped them a bit, but they had to stop frequently, pressing themselves against tree or wall whenever they sensed danger. Keeping close to buildings, they went roughly in the direction of the bathhouse, planning to head for the ramparts after that.

Beyond the bathhouse, Topher took the lead, because he knew the terrain better. It was near where he used to live. He'd played hunting games all over these fields, hunted for real sometimes. He knew where the thickest brambles grew and where the ditches of the old ramparts were deepest. But the rough ground slowed them down. Bent nearly double they came at last to the old ramparts. Topher picked up a stone and tossed it into the inner ditch. Hearing it splash he knew it was too wide to jump over. Better then to follow it southwards, till it got narrower. But soon the tramp of hob-nailed sandals stopped them again and the sky cleared to reveal the moon hanging in the sky like a huge white egg. By its light they saw a legionary on the ramparts, plumed helmet and pointed javelin in sharp relief against the sky.

Flat on the ground, they watched him march past them, northwards towards the east gate. Then they wriggled forward on their stomachs. They were nearly at the narrower part when he turned again – to patrol southwards. Again they lay still as stones. And Topher thanked the gods that the Romans hadn't yet built one of their high walls on top of the ramparts. Getting over the ramparts was going to be difficult enough as it was. Holding their breaths they watched the sentry march past. Then they moved forward again through the undergrowth as quietly as they could, but feeling like wild boars crashing through the forest. Fortunately, the legionary marched on and cloud covered the moon again. But the inner ditch was still too wide to jump. They had to wade through it holding their bundled cloaks above their heads. Then they had to climb the steep slope till at last they were on top of the ramparts. Pressed against the ground they saw a stretch of clear land below them. In daytime sheep grazed there, but now they were safely penned. Beyond was a black mass, the forest, and when the moon appeared again they could see seven tall oak trees higher than the surrounding trees, the sacred circle itself.

The Druid's willow hut was east of that circle, quite a long way east. Silently, Topher begged the gods to help him remember the way to it and recognise it when he saw it. Made of willow wands, it grew out of the ground and was difficult to see, even in daylight, because it looked so much like a bush. He sniffed the air and smelled burnt clay, a sign that they weren't far from the tilemaker's yard, north of them near the east gate. He was in the right place, he was sure of that now. Opposite the tilemaker's yard was a forked tree, an ash, which they must find, for the secret path to the Druid's hut began there. That's where he and Bryn had entered the woods when they'd gone to see him. But first they had to cross that stretch of open country to reach it – on their stomachs or the sentry would surely see them.

Begging the Moon Goddess to hide herself, he led the way down the ramparts and through the ditch at the bottom. Onto their stomachs again. Soaked through now and covered with mud, they wriggled like snakes, but weren't as fast as snakes. Only when the moon was behind cloud could they run – in short stretches, stopping when the patrol came near. Starting again when he had passed.

And they were only half way over when he felt Marcus's hand grip his.

'We're being followed,' Marcus murmured. 'I'm sure of it. Listen.'

They froze and Topher heard a slight rustling behind them. Slowly he turned his head, straining to see in the darkness. Darkness, that was all he could see.

Was Marcus right? It was so easy to imagine things.

Was something following them?

A soldier, a wolf or a bear?

A wild boar or an evil spirit, a bogle, a boggart or a ghost?

Silence again now so they moved forward again.

The rustling again – so they stopped. The something was behind them and it didn't stop. It came closer. Closer. Low to the ground, green eyes gleamed from the darkness. What could it be? Nearer and nearer it came.

Topher froze and held his breath.

Then he felt something rubbing his cheek – something so soft and smooth it could only be one creature – Ca! He breathed again. She must have come out with them, must have been with them all the time! A moonbeam lit up for a moment the ankh on her forehead.

'*Bona fortuna*,' breathed Marcus. 'May the goddess Bastet help us.'

Praying to all the gods that she was a symbol of good luck, Topher turned to face the woods again – and there was a forked tree! Was it the ash he was looking for? The smell of baked clay was stronger. The tilemaker's yard must be behind them.

Bent double now, he headed for the tree, Marcus close behind, the sticky ground sucking their feet as they moved as fast as they could. Was this the stuff that had stuck to Bryn's boots? Had Bryn been this way the night before? Ca didn't like the mud. She streaked ahead in a series of leaps trying to keep her paws above it. They lost sight of her, then saw her green eyes gleaming from the darkness. She was under the tree waiting for them. Between her paws was a bunch of winged ash-seeds.

'You are a good luck sign, Ca. Stay with us.' He stroked her head and she rubbed her cheek against his, then leaped onto his shoulder and clung to his woollen cloak. They would need luck in the forest. Now it was a living presence at their side, a huge monstrous black beast. They could hear it sighing and panting and howling around and above them. They could feel it reaching out with its crooked fingers, sense its huge jaws flexing. Stepping into the wood, Topher half expected teeth to close on him, to rip and chew and tear and destroy him. But he had to go on. It was up to him now.

'May all the dryads of the forest help us,' he heard Marcus murmur.

Ca, clinging to his thick cloak, nestled against his neck. Thank the gods the cat and his friend were with him.

Thank the gods he needed to prove to Marcus that he too was brave or his legs would have buckled beneath him. Beseeching the gods to show him the path, Topher felt his way forward. And the gods answered with scudding clouds and fleeting moonlight, making it slightly easier to see the signs from time to time. An ash branch pointing this way, an oak branch pointing that, a small bush where a deer track forked – he remembered these he thought – but how could he be sure?

Then the ground began to rise – another good sign – though it slowed them down. He pressed on till, after they seemed to have been climbing for hours, a ghostly white figure brought him to a sudden halt. Standing in his path it had long arms and pointing fingers. What was it? A spirit of the walking dead guarding the sacred circle? They must be quite near it now.

Ca's claws dug into his shoulder and Marcus crashed

into his back. For a few moments they clung together, transfixed by the long white finger pointing at them. Then Topher let out his breath, almost laughed, as he realised they were looking at a silver birch tree – its white bark the sign he was looking for. The path to the sacred circle was just behind it.

Now the way became easier. The path led them to the mouth of a tunnel, but that would be even harder to find. Even in the light it had looked like the entrance to a badger set. He came to where he thought it was, near a thicket of alders, felt for it in the darkness. Couldn't find it. Then Ca jumped off his shoulder. A few minutes later he heard her mew. Following the sound he moved to the right – and there it was. She had found the tunnel.

Dark and slimy, this was by far the worst stretch of their journey and seemed to go on forever. Down, down, down they went and then up, they thought, but it was hard to tell. Ca, then Topher, then Marcus crawled through the darkness, till at last Topher thought it was getting lighter.

It was getting lighter!

'You must stay behind when we emerge,' he whispered over his shoulder to Marcus. 'You must not enter the sacred circle. You must wait for me there.'

Even he must not enter it. He would have to skirt its edge as he made his way to the Druid's hut.

Then they were there, cat and two boys in the exit of the tunnel, looking out onto the sacred circle. Towering oaks grew from a pool of silvery moonlight. From their bare branches hung the shrivelled heads of enemies long dead and some less shrivelled, among them the chief of the Catuvellauni killed in the recent battle. It was indeed a holy place. Topher crawled out, taking care not to cross the sacred boundary and slowly stood up. Now he must make his way alone.

'You've got to stay here, exactly here,' he whispered to Marcus. 'And wait for me.'

But before he had moved a muscle, he felt hands clutching his neck.

'Traitor,' hissed a voice he recognised.

Chapter 20

'Why are you here? Why have you brought the Roman?'
Bryn's hands tightened round Topher's neck.

He couldn't speak, could hardly breathe. In front of
him a waterfall seemed to float out of the darkness. It
was some seconds before he realised it was the Druid's
long beard.

'Moon messenger.' The Druid's voice was filled with
awe.

Following his gaze, Topher glimpsed for a second
Ca's eyes gleaming from the mouth of the tunnel. Then
she vanished and his own face hit the mud.

Now Bryn's knee was in Topher's back. 'Why are you
here?' he muttered. 'Have the Romans agreed to our
demands?'

'No. They've got our mother and sisters ... '

'What? Quick. Tell me.' Bryn was binding his wrists.

'I've come for the eagle.'

'It's not here, idiot!'

'Where then?'

'Silence in the sacred place!' The Druid stepped into
the circle. His long white beard flowed down his robes.
'Bind their eyes!'

Then Topher saw no more. Bryn always did what the
Druid said more quickly than most people. He felt
himself jerked to his feet by the thongs round his wrists.

'Where are they?' Bryn murmured in his ear.

125

'Don't know. But they'll be killed if you don't return the eagle,' he managed to say before the Druid ordered them to follow him.

The Druid set a swift pace through the forest. Topher, following blindly, with no hands to steady himself, had to concentrate hard to stay on his feet and avoid bumping into trees. They seemed to walk a long distance, first over springy leaf mould, he thought, then over smoother, harder ground and dry leaves. He felt them beneath his bare feet. And while he walked he listened. There was so much he didn't know. Who else was there? Another adult, he thought. Possibly two as well as Bryn and the Druid. Had Marcus escaped? Probably not. What about Ca? The Druid had been fascinated by her, had called her moon messenger. Had she escaped? He thought perhaps she had but feared for her life in the forest alone.

Suddenly Bryn jerked him to a halt. 'Lower your head.'

Topher ducked as Bryn pushed him forwards.

Then the Druid said, 'Uncover their eyes.'

Though dazzled at first by flickering light, Topher recognised the Druid's round willow hut. In the middle, three torches flared from the mouths of three bronze serpents. Above them, hanging from the roof, a bronze sickle turned slowly, its curved blade gleaming as it caught the light. Shadows danced on the surrounding walls and there stood Marcus. Wyn the smith, looking like a grizzled bear, held his bound wrists.

The Druid pointed to Topher. 'This is your brother?' he said to Bryn.

'It is, holy father.'

'And who is this?' said the Druid, pointing to Marcus who stood to attention, shoulders straight, chin high, every inch a Roman citizen.

'Marcus, the mosaic-maker's son,' said Bryn.

'Come to tell us that the Romans have agreed to our demands?'

Marcus shook his head defiantly, too defiantly, Topher thought.

Bryn said, 'My brother has come to tell us that the Romans have taken our mother and sisters hostage. If we do not return the eagle they say they will kill them.'

'They think we fear death?' said the Druid dismissively.

Topher's heart sank. He should have anticipated this response. The Other Place was what the Druid thought of most, though he seemed in no hurry to go there himself.

'Do the Romans not know,' the Druid went on scornfully, 'that your mother and sisters will welcome death as a passage to another, better world?'

'But...' Topher ignored Bryn's warning thump. 'If the Romans do kill my mother and sisters, because the eagle has not been returned, they will still build the road. Our gods will still be offended. Nothing will be gained.'

'We will have *honour*.' The Druid's eyes burned.

'But our gods will be *dishonoured*,' Topher went on feeling he had nothing to lose. 'The sacred place will still be violated.'

But the Druid wasn't listening. He was saying

something about a bargaining tool. At first Topher didn't understand. Then he heard him say, 'Take this message to the Romans!' He was addressing Bryn and Wyn the smith. 'Tell them we have one of their citizens here. Tell them that if they violate our sacred space the head of Marcus the mosaic-maker's son will hang from our sacred oak! Go! No wait...'

Grasping the sickle, he made a nick in Marcus's mud-covered tunic. Then he ripped off the border. 'Take this with you!'

'I am not afraid to die.' Marcus's voice came out of the gloom.

Alone now, he and Topher were sitting on the floor of another hut. Back to back they were tied together and couldn't see each other, though some early morning light was creeping through the spaces in the woven walls. 'If that is my destiny, I will die bravely.'

Topher thought Marcus sounded far too resigned to his destiny.

'We can *try* to get free,' he said, straining to stretch the thongs round his wrists. 'At least we're alone.' Bryn and Wyn had gone to do the Druid's bidding.

'What about the Druid?' said Marcus gloomily. 'He'll be keeping a lookout. He's in the hut next to this. It's no good. We're doomed. The gods are against us.'

'With a bit of luck the Druid is fast asleep,' Topher replied, flinching as he tried again to free his hands. His wrists felt raw.

'Luck?' said Marcus. 'She seems to have deserted us.

Along with Ca. To think I used to think that cat was lucky.'

Topher tried not to be cast down by his friend's gloomy mood. Fingers of light now reached the middle of the hut and a trill of birdsong broke the silence from time to time. Soon they would be able to see even better, and might even be able to find a sharp stone. If they did, one of them could rub his wrist thongs against it. And they could move a bit, by shuffling on their rears.

'If only we could get our hands free . . . '

'Quiet,' Marcus interrupted. 'There's that noise again.'

Topher stayed still.

They'd heard the noise earlier. At first they'd thought it was a wild animal trying to get in. Then they'd decided it was a branch creaking in the wind. Now it sounded like an animal again.

Scritch scratch.

Scritch scratch.

It went on and on, getting faster.

Scritch scratch. Scritch scratch. He couldn't see anything because it was coming from the dark side of the hut, the west side. They'd taken their bearings when they saw the first streak of light coming through the wattle walls. Then – scraatch scratch – the rhythm changed again. Scraatch scratch. It was stronger now, slightly slower. It wasn't the wind. It was something outside, something that wanted to get in. Some hungry clawed creature had smelt human flesh and wanted an easy meal.

Scraatch scraatch!

Topher felt the bones of his spine press against Marcus's as they both tensed for the attack. Marcus was right after all. Things were going from bad to worse. As light reached the opposite side of the hut, he saw the wall move! Saw it getting thinner. Something was determined to get in. It was shredding the wattle with its claws. Now he couldn't take his eyes off the spot. Fearing for both their lives, he saw the wall give way, saw a paw with claws outstretched! Saw a beautiful face.

'Mwow!'

'Ca!'

She struggled through the hole and took only a moment to greet them both before starting to bite the bonds round Topher's wrists.

Chapter 21

The woods were filled with the sound of waking birds as they crept from the hut. Wriggling through the hole that Ca had begun, they saw why the Romans had never found the Druid who must have fallen asleep. His willow hut, close to the one they were escaping from looked just like a bush. Heading west away from the rising sun, Topher held the exhausted Ca in a fold of his cloak. He had made a sling using a pin borrowed from Marcus. She must have been scratching for hours. Some of her claws were torn and bleeding. But that hadn't stopped her biting through the thongs round Topher's wrists or watching the door, while he helped Marcus break free. Only now as the boys fought their way through the forest, did she sleep. Topher felt her soft body bumping against his. As they speeded up he hoped he wasn't hurting her. Once out of sight and hearing of the huts, they crashed through the forest like hunted hogs, with Topher leading because he knew the forest best.

They didn't try to find the tunnel, partly because it would take too long, partly for fear of getting trapped inside. Instead, with the rising sun as a guide they sought the most direct way through the forest, westwards back to Calleva. Some parts were so dense they couldn't go through them. They had to find another way, following animal tracks whenever they could. They had to reach the city gates before the Druid caught up with them. Had to.

They would be safe then, they hoped. Topher had his doubts. They had disobeyed orders. They hadn't got the eagle. Wouldn't the soldiers on the gate arrest them, if they hadn't rained spears on them on sight? He wished he had time to stop and think. Where had Bryn hidden the eagle? Finding it was more important than ever now. Only finding it might break the deadlock. As he pushed back branches and unhooked himself from brambles he thought how futile the conflict was.

Roman honour versus Atrebatan honour.

Roman power versus Atrebatan power. Neither side would give in. Result – death and bloodshed. Why couldn't they settle their differences as he and Marcus had done. Glancing back at his friend, he saw his neat head held high. He still looked like a Roman despite his torn clothes and the mud and leaves sticking to him. Seeing Topher, he gave the thumbs-up sign and grinned.

And Topher began to feel more hopeful. So far so good. There was still no sign of the Druid and there were spaces between the trees now. So they must be nearing the edge of the woods. He'd found their way this far, thanks be to the gods. They were lucky. All things began to seem possible, even persuading Bryn to tell him where the eagle was. Marcus said the Romans would have arrested him and Wyn the smith when they delivered their ultimatum. So Topher must get to them fast. Away from the Druid Bryn would tell him, surely? He wouldn't let his mother and sisters be killed.

'Topher! Lady Luck is with us I think!' Marcus, by his side now, was pointing ahead. Topher followed his gaze. And there was the V-shaped ash! They had arrived at the point where they had entered the forest. And there was the field beyond, shining with sunlight, and beyond that the city gates! Pausing for a moment, they leaned against the ash tree, watching a soldier on the ramparts, his spear and helmet gleaming in the morning sun.

'*Salve!*' yelled Marcus, thought his voice was unlikely to carry that far. '*Salve!*'

Then holding up their hands to make it clear they had no weapons, they stepped out of the woods and began to walk towards the closed gates – and got no reaction! None at all. The soldier, who was looking straight at them, didn't seem to see them. In fact, they soon realised, he couldn't see them because they were walking in the shadow of the forest – and he was staring straight into the sun. It was blinding him. As they tramped towards him, wondering whether to shout again – might he throw a spear before asking questions? – the soldier turned away from them and began to march southwards.

Now the ground beneath their feet was sticky and Topher remembered the clay on Bryn's boots the night he returned from stealing the eagle. The tilemaker's yard was to their right. Bryn *had* been this way – he'd guessed right about that – but he hadn't taken the eagle to the Druid. So where had he hidden it? Stopping to scrape some of the clay off his feet with a stick, Topher observed rows and rows of big cubes of wet clay, ranged in front of some buildings. *Big cubes of wet clay!* What a superb hiding place one of them would make! Would Bryn have had that thought? Suddenly Topher thought that he might. There were about twenty cubes, all covered with damp cloths. The tileyard seemed deserted too. Had it been deserted when Bryn went by? There was no sign of a guard now. There were some makeshift buildings though, where someone might be hidden. *But Bryn could have come here at night unobserved. Could have buried the eagle in one of the cubes of clay!* It had to be worth a look. Ca seemed to think so too. She stirred and poked her head out of his cloak, and made a soft chirruping sound, but then went back to sleep.

Marcus took a bit of persuading. He was keen to get inside the town. Topher still had his doubts. What if they were arrested? He had disobeyed orders. People might not believe in their good intentions. *But if they walked in with the eagle* ... He pictured to Marcus how wonderful that would be and a few minutes later they were both in the tileyard, casting their eyes over the big cubes of clay.

'So which one?' Marcus still looked doubtful. 'We can't pull them all apart to see if the eagle is inside. It would take ages.'

Topher said, 'First, let's lift the cloths to see if any of them are marked. You start that end. I'll start this.'

He'd looked at six – none of them with any distinguishing marks – and was feeling a bit gloomy when Ca stirred again. He saw one of her paws sticking out from his cloak. Was she pointing?

'Is it this one, Ca?' He lifted the cloth covering the block in front of him. There was a tiny swirl in the corner. When he thrust into the clay with a stick, he felt something hard!

'Marcus, come over here!'

But Marcus couldn't move.

He could hear, but couldn't see Topher because his eyes were turned skywards.

The Druid – where had he come from? – held the sickle against his throat.

Chapter 22

'Bring the eagle to me!' The Druid's lilting voice was soft but unmistakable. Clearly he didn't want to rouse the guard at the gate.

Terribly, terribly aware of the danger to Marcus, Topher tried desperately to think. As he dug into the clay with his fingers, heads hanging from trees flashed into his mind. What should he do for the best? Sticky clay stuck to his fingers, as he tried to prise the block apart. Had he got any bargaining power? Would the Druid exchange the life of Marcus for the eagle?

'Quickly!' The Druid seemed agitated as he bent Marcus's neck further back, bringing the blade closer.

Now Topher could feel the shape of a wing beneath his fingers. Within seconds the eagle could be in his hands. What then? Should he hand it over straightaway? Say 'I'll give it to you if you let Marcus go?' Why hadn't anyone from the town noticed what was happening? Was the soldier on the ramparts blind? Were the guards in the gatehouse asleep?

As he considered the alternatives a trumpet sounded.

At first he thought it was from the town.

Then he realised it wasn't, for the Druid was looking over his shoulder. The sound was coming from behind him.

Taran ta taa! Who was blowing the trumpet?

'Hurry, boy!'

Trying to look as if he was hurrying, Topher played for time.

What was going on? The trumpet sounded again, louder now. It was coming from the northeast, from the heathland to the north of the forest, where there was a road – but only to some gravel pits. And there was another sound accompanying it, a lower, more constant sound, a humming sound. Now he noticed that all the birds had gone quiet. The trees had gone quiet. It was as if they were listening too, as if everything was listening – to the hum getting louder, louder, coming closer, closer. Topher's hopes began to rise. Flicking clay off his fingers, he risked another glance at Marcus as the trumpet sounded again, and a trumpet from the city gates answered with a loud fanfare. The Druid, agitated, looked over his shoulder again, but still had Marcus in his grasp. The sound didn't please him.

Taran-tata! Taran-tataa!

Taran-taran!

Taran-tata!

'Hurry, boy!' Now the Druid roared and Topher delved into the clay again, working as quickly as he could. Pulling handfuls of clay from the eagle embedded in the block, he hurled them onto the ground. But eyes squinting against the sun, he still glanced up from time to time to see what the Druid was doing, and to search the landscape. And at last he saw the cause of the Druid's agitation and his own hopes. For moving towards them from the northeast, over the heath, was a dark column. A long, dark column was snaking towards them. For the hum, more of a throb now, was the low rhythm of a jaunty marching song! Soldiers, Roman legionaries, hundreds of them, their spears like a moving forest, were approaching fast!

Taran-tata!

Taran-taran!

As the trumpets from town replied to those of the approaching army Topher's heart leaped! Relief, the same relief he'd felt on the morning of the battle with the Catuvellauni, when he'd seen the Romans rising from the mist, flooded him. But then he heard the Druid roaring, 'The eagle, boy! Now!'

And realising that Marcus could be dead before the army arrived, he pulled hard on the eagle. With a massive *schluck* it came out of the clay and he held it above his head!

'Help me, Ca. I need your help.'

She was still beneath his cloak.

'He thinks you're a messenger from the Moon Goddess, so do your stuff. Wise one, look!'

Holding the eagle high and praying to the Moon Goddess, the goddess Fortuna, the goddess Bastet and all the gods he could think of, he began to walk forwards steadily till he was standing in front of the Druid. Then he sank to his knees, put the eagle at his feet and spoke into the old man's long white beard, 'Wise one, I have a message from the Moon Goddess!'

Then he looked up, lifting back his cloak to reveal Ca.

And the Druid looked down with amazement.

Topher could not see, but knew that Ca's eyes were

shining as if from a dark cave. The Druid was gazing into the twin moons of Ca's eyes.

'This messenger from the Moon Goddess aided our escape!' said Topher, turning slightly so that the sun reached Ca's eyes. 'See her moon-eyes waxing and waning!'

He then turned back into the shadow created by the Druid.

And as the Druid leaned closer to see, so of course did Marcus, for the Druid still held him firmly. But there was hope in his friend's brown eyes.

'See her claws like sacred sickles!' Topher went on, gently pressing the soft pad of one forepaw.

The Druid leaned forward to examine them. 'This creature aided your escape?'

'Yes, wise one. She released us from our bonds. Can you tell us why?'

As Ca put out a paw and caught a tendril of the Druid's white beard, Topher held his breath.

It was quiet now. No singing. No marching feet. Had the Roman army passed by? As the seconds passed Topher could see the Druid thinking. But what was he thinking as he studied the white hairs in Ca's sickle-shaped claws?

'What does it mean, O wise one? What does the Moon Goddess want of us?'

As Topher waited for an answer, he saw from the corner of his eye a purple-cloaked Roman on a chestnut stallion, the red plume of his helmet quivering. Behind this man – a general, Topher thought – were hundreds of

Roman legionaries, their spears glinting in the sunlight. Then Topher saw someone else, almost hidden by the Roman leader. He saw his *father* on horseback. His *father*, looking somewhat thinner and browner, but unmistakably his father, chief of the tribe with his long fair hair and plaid cloak. He saw his father dismount and walk slowly towards the Druid, who still held the knife against Marcus's throat.

'Wise one,' said Bryn the Elder softly. 'I bring good news – that the sacred grove is safe. Wise one, the sacred grove will not be violated.'

The Druid looked up.

'Wise one, I have the word of Agricola, Governor General of Britannia.' He gestured towards the purple-cloaked man on horseback. 'The sacred site of the Moon Goddess will be respected. The road to the east will be built elsewhere.'

In the moments that followed a blackbird trilled from a tree in the woods. Its song penetrated the silence, which hung like taut threads between watchers and watched.

What would the Druid do? As they waited Topher saw a nerve jumping beneath the old man's left eye. Then he saw his arm slowly descend.

Marcus stooped to pick up the eagle.

Then he carried it to the Governor his head held high!

Chapter 23

Topher would never forget the rejoicing. He heard the cheers coming from the Forum, even though he was some distance away. He was in the roundhouse, sitting at the feet of his father, hearing about his long quest to seek justice for his people.

'*Euge! Euge!*' the crowd roared when the eagle was returned to its rightful place in the hand of the Emperor. And Bryn the Elder paused for a moment.

The rejoicing in the compound was more restrained. It was hard to forget the havoc wrought by the soldiers searching for the eagle. But recompense had been made – on the orders of the Governor. Buildings had been mended, goods replaced. Most importantly, the fire in the roundhouse had been rekindled.

They sat round the fire now, as Bryn continued the tale of his travels. He'd been first to Noviomagus, to the palace of King Cogidubnus, only to find he was not there! Cogidubnus had gone to visit Governor Agricola in the capital. So Bryn the Elder had ridden north to the capital, Camulodunum, where he was granted an audience with Agricola the Governor. Fortunately the Governor had seen the justice of his case. Realising the danger in Calleva, he'd ordered the fourth legion to prepare to leave immediately, and they had all set off with Agricola at their head. Bryn the Elder had ridden at his side. Moving at military speed, they were still twenty miles from Calleva – after three days' marching – when they met the magistrates' messenger, and learned of the theft of the eagle. Determined to avert a disaster, Agricola had urged the legion to carry on marching through the night even though they had marched twenty miles that day. Topher knew the rest, but listened to it anyway, happy that peace and order and warmth had been restored.

And three days later they rejoiced together. Romans, Romano-Atrebatans and Atrebatans from the compound. First they celebrated in the morning with games and races in the amphitheatre. Then they celebrated again, in the Basilica, at a banquet in honour of Agricola. Some Atrebatans refused the invitation. Bryn the Younger and Wyn the smith were still in prison awaiting trial, but at sunset Topher and the rest of his family put on their finest robes and ornaments and set off for the feast. Topher thought his mother and sisters looked beautiful with their shining braided hair and long tunics dyed bluebell blue. He was proud too of himself, dressed like his father in a russet tunic and a swishing cloak fixed on the shoulder by a bronze brooch in the swirling British style. He had a moment's worry, on the steps of the Basilica, when he saw the Roman guests arriving, because they all carried their eating tools wrapped in white cloths, but then he saw Marcus who said, 'Don't worry, we've brought extra for you.'

Then Cassius and Bryn the Elder greeted each other warmly with man to man hugs, and they entered the Basilica together. How different it was from the last time

Topher had been there. Now, long tables on three sides of the room were piled high with food! So much food! So many different *kinds* of food! So many different *containers* of food! Topher had never seen so much food in his life. There were serving dishes shaped like sheep and cows so you expected sheep meat or cow meat but got something completely different. There were fruit bowls shaped like fountains with waterfalls of grapes, and there was red wine from curvy fat amphorae and pink wine from curvy thin amphorae. Food and drink had been brought from all over the Roman Empire Marcus said, for their delight and the Governor's of course. At first Topher couldn't see Governor Agricola. Then Marcus pointed him out, just getting to his feet, behind the top table. A row of slaves stood behind him. Agricola raised his arms to heaven, called upon the gods to attend their feast and then lay down again.

Eating lying down, with the white cloth tucked under your chin, took a bit of getting used to. So did some of the dishes, stuffed dormice for instance with fish sauce, and snails fried in oil, but lots of it was delicious. The roast boar, baked crisp with an apple in its mouth, tasted of honey and ginger and a herb called rosemary. The stewed venison in its sauce of lovage and coriander made your mouth water. Pheasant and peacock's eggs slipped down your throat. There was so *much* food and when you thought you were finished – there was even more. Slaves cleared the tables. Acrobats and jugglers performed amazing feats in the middle of the room. Then slaves brought in *more* dishes – even sweeter ones!

Stuffed dates and honeyed omelettes, honeyed wine cakes tasting of aniseed and cumin, almond cakes and pears cooked in wine and cinnamon, sweet chestnuts in honey and fennel sauce and more sweet red wine.

Topher ate and drank so much he thought he might burst or be sick, like some of the Romans who *were* sick – into bowls held by slaves – and then went back to eat even more! He was quite relieved when Marcus said, 'Come outside, friend Topher, I want to tell you something.'

The leaf-fall air was cool, the silence of the night a blissful relief from the noise inside. The two boys stood on the Basilica steps for a moment, looking up at the full moon and the gleaming patterns of stars. Then something made Topher look down at the Forum square bathed in the moon's silvery light – and there was Ca, sitting at the base of the imperial statue. Vespasian was there and so was the imperial eagle. Peace reigned and all was well. Tomorrow the tribe would go to the sacred grove and worship the Moon Goddess. Marcus said he would make an offering to Diana, the Romans' moon goddess.

'We're going home, Topher.' His voice broke the silence. 'As soon as we've finished the bathhouse floors – in a few days' time. That's what I have to tell you. And we want you to have Ca,' he said in a rush and the cat looked round.

Then she started to walk towards them, casting a long cat-shadow across the square. 'We would like you to look after her for us, till we return,' Marcus went on as they watched her coming towards them, tail held high. 'She's having kittens, we think, and the journey wouldn't be good for her. We don't know what we'll find when we reach Pompeii.' His voice tailed off.

Ca stood between them now, rubbing first Marcus's leg, then Topher's.

'She likes you so much,' said Marcus. 'Will you look after her for us?'

'Of course I will.' Topher gathered the wonderful animal into his arms and buried his face in her fur.

'I'll go and tell Pater then,' said Marcus running up the steps.

Topher said he would wait outside with Ca.

'What were you looking at, cat? What *are* you looking at?' She seemed to be looking at the moon. 'Are you a messenger from the Moon Goddess?' For several moments he stood with her in his arms, following her gaze. Then he saw something else in the eastern sky, a golden shooting star! Ca was watching it too.

The star was crossing the sky diagonally, shooting towards them at a terrific speed. But it wasn't an ordinary shooting star he saw, as it got closer. It was a bird-shaped star. No, it was a bird, a golden bird! He could see it now almost directly above them, hear its swishing wings, see those wings pulling back to slow itself, see its feet dangling. For a moment the bird seemed to hang in the air, then down it came!

Down came horny-scaled feet and dark breast. Casting a shadow over them. Cutting off the light from the moon.

Down, down came a magnificent golden eagle onto the steps of the Basilica. They could see the dark golden ridge along the leading edge of its great wings, see the long pinions, the folded claws and the head with its powerful beak, sunk into its shoulders. Then boy, cat and eagle were bathed in moonlight on the Basilica steps as the bird seemed to survey the square. Looking down Topher saw its fanned tail spread out towards him, and the shawl of golden feathers at the base of its neck. Then the huge neck swung round and a hook-beak faced boy and cat. Black-rimmed golden eyes glared.

'Eek!'

Ca ran up the tail onto the bird's back.

'Eek!'

Topher followed, clinging to the bird's springy feathers as he pulled himself up to the top. Then he slid down into the hollow of its back where Ca was waiting. The eagle swung round to face forwards. Topher positioned himself, kneeling with Ca between his knees. Then he put his arms round the eagle's strong neck as the bird's body tensed. Wings rose on either side, there was a rush of air through fur and hair as they rose and fell, then they were off! Cat and boy held on tight as the bird climbed rapidly and suddenly Calleva was a chequerboard beneath them, the squares getting smaller and smaller as the bird climbed higher and higher. Whooshing wings beat faster and faster and faster! Then with Calleva behind them and star-filled darkness around them, the bird's wings stopped beating. The eagle soared at unbelievable speeds through space and time, while Ca and Topher slept.

*

When they woke the bird's wings were moving again. It was pulling back, braking. Looking down, Topher saw another chequered pattern of roads beneath him. For a moment he thought he was back in Calleva, then as the eagle flew lower he glimpsed for a second a block of flats, a TV aerial and the Market Cross of Chichester. Then he was landing on the porch of Fletcher House, where there was a lot of activity in the garden below. A car zoomed into the drive and his father got out.

'Topher, are you all right?'

'How did you get up there?'

Topher looked for the eagle but it wasn't there. He looked for Ka – who was there – at his feet!

Then blue lights flashed as an ambulance zoomed into the drive, followed by a police car. People were pointing in various directions. People were moving in various directions. Ambulance men moved to the still body below the porch. A knife lay about a metre away. Policemen approached the crouching bodies at the gate.

'Topher, come inside.' This time his father's voice came from behind him. He helped Topher climb through the broken window onto the landing, helped him step carefully over the broken glass.

Chapter 24

'There's not a lot to see,' said Ellie. 'It looks more like a football pitch than a town.'

'Football pitches don't have seven sides,' Topher replied, but he had to agree it was hard to believe that the field in front of them was once a town called Calleva. It was several months since he'd returned from his trip back in time. He and Ellie were standing on the wall which now went right round the town. Made of stones, the bit they were on was about a metre wide and three metres high. It was near the west gateway and a track stretched out in front of them. At the far end of it, where the east gate once stood, was a grey stone church with a tower and a couple of very un-Roman brick houses.

From the ramparts below came his dad's voice, fussing over Tallulah, the new baby. She had black hair, a round face nearly as red as the sling Molly was carrying her in, and she was fast asleep, but his dad was worrying whether it would be too windy for her if they walked along the top. It wasn't cold, not at all. The sun was shining in fact, but a breeze shook the golden dandelions, which dotted the grass.

'Are there really Roman streets under that lot?' said Ellie, scrunching up her face and shaking her head.

'Yes and pavements and buildings with mosaic floors,' Topher replied, seeing them vividly in his mind's eye. They'd seen a lot of Roman stuff in Reading Museum, earlier that day. The rest really was under all that grass. In the museum they'd seen a well-shaft, lots of pots and part of a mosaic floor – but not the dolphin mosaic that Topher most wanted to see. Could that still be under the grass? He pictured the bathhouse to the right of where they were now. They'd seen coins, leather sandals, and the bronze eagle wingless now, but best of all, they'd seen Ka's pawprint in the terracotta tile!

'Ka did that,' he'd said and Ellie had laughed. He didn't try to explain.

It was May half-term and she was staying with them. They'd had a good lunch in the Calleva Arms at Silchester, a village about a mile from Calleva. Now they were going to walk round the walls.

'You can see why they chose to build a town here,' Ellie said. 'It's higher than the surrounding land. You can see people approaching for miles.'

They were in the middle of a patchwork of fields, with most patches the dayglo-yellow of oilseed rape.

'Not then you couldn't,' he replied, still seeing it in his mind's eye. 'It was surrounded by forest then, except for a strip round the ramparts.' He pointed to the track. 'I think that follows the old east-west road.'

'So where was the Forum?' asked Ellie.

'Straight ahead, in the middle of the field, to the right a bit, though you wouldn't have been able to see it from here. The Basilica was in the way. It formed the west side. There were shops on the other three sides and a statue of the Emperor Vespasian in the middle. He was

149

holding the eagle, the one we saw in the museum.'

'You're very knowledgeable about the Romans, Topher. Have you turned into a swot?' She looked at him suspiciously.

'You're very knowledgeable about babies,' he said. 'As you should be.'

'Sexist!' She pushed him dangerously near the edge of the wall.

'But you were so right,' he went on. 'About babies. Tallulah is okay, just as you said. Smelly sometimes but okay and Molly adores her. So does my dad. He even changes her nappy sometimes.'

They were still fussing round her. Then his dad called out, 'We're going to walk southwards, outside the walls, to get a bit of protection from the wind.' He was helping Molly and the baby down the grassy slope. 'You two do what you want. We'll meet in the churchyard, round the other side, in about half an hour!'

'It is natural to feel a bit jealous in these circumstances,' said Ellie as she and Topher watched them, before setting off in the opposite direction.

'Well I'm unnatural,' he replied. 'I like Tally a lot. I'm just glad they like her too.'

'What does Ka think of her babies now?'

Ka had had four kittens.

'She's very proud of them but I think she'll be glad when I find homes for some of them at least. They're getting very lively now, so she doesn't get much rest.'

'I'm longing to see them, but I'm not so keen on meeting this new friend of yours.'

'Brett Durno?'

'Yes, your former enemy. The one who tried to drown you.' Ellie frowned. 'Are you sure you can trust him?'

As they walked past the north gate, where the roundhouse used to be, Topher tried to explain. 'Brett didn't try to drown me. He hated me because I moved into Fletcher House, which he still thought of as his home. He had to leave it when his dad went off. And he found himself next door to Ring-lip as it happened. For a short time, he tagged along with him and his crowd. He even tried glue-sniffing...'

'That's no reason...'

'No, but...anyway, don't interrupt, Ellie...we've sorted things out.'

They'd had to sort things. Mr Trustram had been so impressed by the way they'd worked together in a difficult situation, that he made them crew-mates. They sailed a lot together now, had won a few contests in fact, and you couldn't do that if you were enemies. You simply have to work together in a boat. And – Topher had checked up on this – Brett really didn't know that the Arno gang was going to follow him home that night. He'd been trying to distance himself from them, ever since he'd realised what they were really like and how he was becoming like them. He'd been shocked when he found out what they'd done.

'Well, I think you're very forgiving,' said Ellie.

'You've got to be,' said Topher, and Ellie muttered something about his halo.

They were standing on the northeast wall now, near

where he had watched the Catuvellauni tribe bearing down on the Atrebatans with their spears and flaming torches. He remembered how he'd once hated Marcus because he was a Roman, and how they had become best friends.

'What's the point of bearing grudges?' he went on. 'What's the point of tribalism and fighting to the death? Of racism and revenge. You've only got to look at the news to see what happens when people carry on wars their ancestors started hundreds of years ago. It's crazy. We've got to learn to get on together.'

'You're right of course,' said Ellie, linking her arm in his. 'I want to save the world too, not just whales.' She was wearing a faded Save the Whale t-shirt. 'Now let's look over there.' She pointed to the amphitheatre outside the walls.

It was much as he remembered it from that last morning, except that it was quiet now and empty. The walls round the arena were still intact. He remembered the cheering crowds in the tiered seats, the runners and the charioteers and the wrestling matches, the mood of celebration.

'This is good,' Ellie said as they stepped inside the arena. 'Do you think they had gladiatorial combats here?'

'I don't think they had many in Britain.' He didn't remember seeing any. 'They did like to see wild animals fighting though. And they had races here, all sorts of races. I suppose it was a cross between a circus and a sports stadium really, but crueller. There was probably an ... ' A shiver ran through him as the word execution came into his mouth, and he wondered what had happened to Bryn. He was glad he hadn't been around to see. He had never witnessed one himself but the Romans did behead traitors or worse, crucify them. They had a lot of good qualities but they weren't into forgiveness.

'Let's get back on the walls,' he said. 'I'll race you to the churchyard.'

Opposite the churchyard in the middle of a sea of dazzling yellow was a copse of tall trees. Oak trees? Could that be the site of the sacred grove? He couldn't be sure, but for a second he saw it vividly, saw the scene darken, saw the tall trees by moonlight, saw white skulls hanging like lamps from their branches.

Tallulah's yells were a welcome intrusion.

Ellie said, 'Here's the rest of the family.'

But Topher was already walking to meet them. His dad called out, 'We're going into the church so that Molly can sit and feed Tally.' Fortunately the door wasn't locked and when Tallulah stopped screaming, it was very peaceful.

'Do you know what I want to do next,' said Ellie as they sat on a pew together.

'What?'

'Go home, to your posh new house.' She linked her arm with his. 'I want to see Ka and her kittens.'

Ka was in the conservatory watching pink petals fall from the cherry tree in the garden. Her four plump kittens were sleeping in a box.

153

'Uno, Duo, Tres and Zingi,' Topher said, pointing to a black kitten, two tabbies and a ginger one in turn. The tabbies and the ginger each had a faint ankh on their foreheads. 'One, Two, Three and Ginger – in Latin,' he explained.

'I'm keeping Zingi, the ginger one. He's a tom. The new owners can re-name them if they want I suppose.'

'I'm having this one,' said Ellie, picking up Duo, 'and I shall keep her name.'

Topher said Brett was coming round later that evening to choose his. Ka came over to investigate, then jumped in the box and started to wash behind Zingi's ears. He woke up and started to climb out of the box. She took him by the scruff of his neck and finished washing his ears.

'They're gorgeous,' said Ellie, putting Duo back in the box. 'But it's a pity that none of them looks exactly like Ka.'

'Ka's unique,' said Topher, as she stretched out to feed her kittens. She began to purr and he was suffused with gladness – that he lived where and when he did. It was good to visit the past, but not to live there. You have to move on.

Rrrr...Rrr...

You're right, Topher.

'I'm glad you think so, Ka,' said Topher.

ABOUT THE AUTHOR

Julia Jarman lives in a north Bedfordshire village with her husband and Perdita the cat – an inspiration! She loves visiting schools and libraries to do talks about her stories. Urged to write by her three children ("Write about children like us – and put lots of scary bits in!), she has written twelve novels for Andersen Press, including the Time-Travelling Cat series.

She likes pigs and plays, cats and computers, food – growing, cooking and eating it – and books.

For more info visit her happy, zappy, snappy website www.juliajarman.com